Occam's Dream

A Novel

Previous Works:

Death Lines: Walking London's Horror History
ISBN 1913689387

Occam's Dream

A Novel

Lauren Jane Barnett

London, UK
Washington, DC, USA

First published by Roundfire Books, 2025
Roundfire Books is an imprint of Collective Ink Ltd.,
Unit 11, Shepperton House, 89 Shepperton Road, London, N1 3DF
office@collectiveinkbooks.com
www.collectiveinkbooks.com
www.roundfire-books.com

For distributor details and how to order please visit the 'Ordering' section on our website.

ISBN: 978 1 80341 719 6
978 1 80341 732 5 (ebook)
Library of Congress Control Number: 2023950375

A CIP catalogue record for this book is available from the British Library.

Design: Lapiz Digital Services

UK: Printed and bound by CPI Group (UK) Ltd, Croydon, CR0 4YY
Printed in North America by CPI GPS partners

For Dean & Kathy

Contents

Ursula

Today needs to be a good day.

Phommm. The thought was punctuated by a gentle, resonant thud.

"Huh?" Ursula mumbled, as much to herself as to the succulent seated on the bookshelf.

She put down the ceramic cup of water she had been feeding the plant and walked to the window. The thought crossed her mind of a bird; its body glancing off the glass.

She scanned the floor-length window for any sign of where the sound came from. All she saw were the rows of roofs beyond, jig-sawing their way down to the grey ocean and matching hazy sky. Running her hands over the smooth surface, she couldn't detect any change invisible to the eye. The only marks were where her fingerprints smudged the pane. She swallowed, sending a popping through her ears.

There was nothing. Why would there be?

With a sigh, she stepped back and examined the window again. Behind a wall of clouds, the round white glow of the sun stared back at her like a judgemental drowned eye. Under the glare, Ursula wondered if the sound had been in her head.

It wouldn't be the first time.

No, Ursula commanded herself. She wasn't going to consider that. It had been almost a year. She had to trust herself now. After all, the company did. At least, enough to let her return.

"Let's hope that isn't an omen, Herb," she commented, glancing over her shoulder. The succulent smiled back at her from its perch on the bookcase, the pink edges glowing in contented peace. Evidently, Herb didn't think there was anything to worry about.

"It was nothing," Ursula insisted to herself. "I'm sure I'm just anxious getting back to work."

She felt foolish saying it out loud. Herb sat quietly and took it all in, but he must be bored of her already. Herb had been hearing about work for as long as she had been caring for him; two days into medical leave. She had mentioned it almost every day for eight months.

It had helped, talking to Herb. When her therapist had suggested it, Ursula was certain it would be pointless. Technically, Jill had suggested Ursula get a pet, but in those first weeks she was barely in a state to clean herself, let alone feed and care for a pet. Jill handed her a succulent, explaining that she didn't need to water it every day. It could take care of itself until Ursula was ready.

Secretly, Ursula had expected him to die months ago. Yet, from the start, there had been something appealing about Herb. He gave her a feeling of nostalgic comfort, as though she'd had one in childhood.

Not that her memory had recovered enough to know that. Maybe it had been that familiarity, or maybe it had been the circumstances – stuck in the empty apartment, unable to stand from the dizziness of anxiety – but she talked to Herb from the first day. And look at her now: ready to go back to work.

Mostly ready.

"Where was I?" Ursula asked aloud to stifle her sneaking uneasiness.

She turned back to the room, her feet naturally moving to the greying spot that marked her usual place. With the anticipation of peace, she settled down on the plush, white carpet. She smiled at the sensation of the fibres curving to cradle her crossed thighs. The act of sitting caused the muscles around her neck to unfurl, ready for her daily anchor of meditation.

She rested her eyes on the centre of the window, taking in the expansive ocean that formed a background to her view. Her heart gave a grateful shudder. Her vision unfixed to take in the expansive greying blue. In a few minutes, she could face the world again. The first inhale lifted her chest, straightening her back. The exhale trickled over her shoulders and down her back. At the second breath, she could sense her mind loosening, lulled by the rhythmic rise and fall of her body. On the third exhale, she felt a distant tingle in her toes before she closed her eyes.

Five seconds in, hold for one, and six seconds out.

With each count the thought of the thud against the windowpane faded; as did the hopes for the day, the dullness of the sky, the ageing white of her meditation room, and that perpetual tug behind her ribs. The nerves, the doubt, the months of therapy and exercises, all softened into a distant buzz. The rolling wave of breath took over, and she relaxed into the stillness.

In.

And out.

In –

CRACK.

Her mind twisted and split. The sound was sucked from her ears.

A bright, harsh yellow ruptured the darkness of her eyelids. Her heart stopped. Her lungs halted. A single image seized her in a violent visual grip: a wide, dusty, expanse suspended beneath an unforgiving pale sky. The jaundiced desert scorched her mind. An unbearable feverish heat smothered her, and her eardrums pulsed against a rapid swell of pressure. She felt an excruciating stab just above her left eyebrow. The force and precision of it felt like being shot.

Her eyes flew open.

She tried to scream but there was no air in her lungs. Her mind scattered searching for her heart and willing it to beat. By some miracle it did. The movement forced her mouth open in a gasp, and she scraped air into her lungs in a laboured breath. Her heart thudded, lurching in her chest like a frantic animal. Each individual blood cell strained for oxygen.

After a few wheezing breaths, her muscles seemed to recover and her body became familiar once more. Somewhere in the aftermath sound had returned to her ears. She could hear the wretched drawl of her broken breaths, and the pounding of her heartbeat overlaying a faint distant hum of the ocean. She latched onto the sound and it carried her back.

The world around her reassembled in pieces, beginning with the horizon line of the ocean. The rough texture of the carpet returned, prickling her sensitive skin. The heat of her body jarred against the chilly air. The curdling sick rising in her throat.

She swallowed and it held back.

Her trembling fingers found the spot above her left eyebrow that had, for the briefest of seconds, stung with blinding force. She could only liken it now to an ice-pick being driven through her skull. The skin was burning, but there was no sign of blood.

I'm alive, she reminded herself. *I'm okay.* A rush of tingles spread over her body, falling in a gentle but swift cascade.

Forcing her mind away from the shadow of pain, she turned to the image that had come with it. Though it had only appeared for a moment, the details sprung vividly to mind: a barren, cracked desert stretched out beneath a faded sky, broken by a single train of dust curling up in the wind like Death's beckoning finger.

Ursula shuddered. A tingling ran over her legs.

What if it was a stroke?

She jostled her muscles into a swift, aching smile. Her false grin stretched evenly on both sides. She thrust out her arms, fingers splayed and straight. Carefully, she examined them. The skin was paler than usual, making the twist of blue veins in her hands stand out, but they were steady, and level.

A gasping laugh burst out of her. It wasn't a stroke. Her breath returned – when had she stopped breathing? – and her hands started to tremble.

Ursula had never been to a desert, but she had seen them on film and in dreams. This one seemed crueller: a skeletal corpse of land bleached by unforgiving sunshine. Somehow the harsh reminder sent an icy chill through her body. She watched as the skin on her arms raised into a tiny forest of bumps. Her eyes followed the gooseflesh as it spread over her skin until it became lost under the smooth plastic black band of her watch.

As if it sensed her though, the band glowed blue with the time. 7:42.

She leapt before she could think and ran to the shower. She couldn't miss her train, not today.

***

"So, you have returned to the wild city," Rob greeted her with a smile.

Ursula's shoulders jumped. Her mind had been skittering over the morning, still unable to anchor onto what happened. For a moment she stared, uncertain how long her friend had been standing there.

"Hi," Ursula replied, blinking too many times. She could hear the stiffness in her own voice.

"Sorry. My mind was somewhere else," she continued. Why couldn't she form full sentences? She shook her head, trying to shed the morning.

"Are you doing okay?" Rob asked. The sun twinkled on his brilliant white teeth contrasting with his skin. His smile always felt personal, specially designed for each person he showed it to. The sight of it, and the kind concern in his eyes steadied her.

"Yes." For a moment she considered telling him. But she didn't want to relive it. Or ruin his morning.

"I just can't believe I'm finally back." Immediately, her stomach clenched. Why had she said that? Rob had been the only connection with work while she was isolated. He had heard at least as much as Herb how desperately she wanted to be back. She told him the day she was given the all-clear to return. She should have been thanking him for meeting her at the front, not pointing out the obvious.

Wait – why was he there? They hadn't planned it.

"You were getting impatient," Rob commented, cutting off her question. "How are things at the seaside retirement home?"

Ursula forced down the wave of defensive replies that surged up from her lungs and rolled her eyes.

"The sea is still beautiful," Ursula replied pointedly. "You should come back out some weekend."

He may have talked about thriving on the movement of people and the overflow of faces in the city, but she never saw him smile so widely as when they walked along the beach together.

"I am due," Rob agreed. "It's been what – six weeks since I last visited?"

"Longer."

"It couldn't be. I saw you last month when I got promoted."

"Here," Ursula reminded him. "My train was delayed, and you told the waitress you thought you were being stood up. Thanks again for that."

"I got a free drink," he laughed.

"And the month before that, you had to cancel last minute. You haven't been out to see me for at least two months."

"Oh, that is bad," Rob admitted. He wrinkled his nose in disappointment. Ursula smiled. He looked like a bear who swallowed unripe fruit.

"It's hard to keep track lately," Rob continued. "We're updating the security system and since I am the newest team manager, I am stuck leading the weekend teams."

"It's okay. When you do get time, though, you are always welcome." Ursula felt a flitter in the back of her mind. She suddenly felt she had been too dismissive. If she was more insistent, he probably would visit more often. She should have said she missed him; but the moment had passed.

"Wait, does that mean that you haven't done anything social in two months?" Rob smirked.

"I walk on the beach almost every day," Ursula shot back.

"Alone. When did you last go out to a restaurant?"

"Thursday, actually," Ursula retorted. "And that's also something I can do on my own. In fact, I make good company."

Rob chuckled and flashed his pass to the security guard at the gate. The tall woman pushed a button and the barrier opened. As they passed through, Ursula realised that he was escorting her like a guest.

Her hand automatically went to the card jammed in her pocket. Had they rescinded her security clearance?

"Well maybe now that you are back in the workforce you can do things with real people," Rob continued. "Go to a movie after work or maybe to a real-live bar?"

"Or *maybe* I'll take you out if you ever visit me again," she countered.

"Ouch," he put his hand over his heart in mock despair. "Fair enough; but at least I text."

"You absolutely do," Ursula laughed.

Rob almost always texted in the middle of the night, knowing full well that Ursula was asleep. The next morning, she would wake up to a series of questions or comments ranging from 'oh my god this is so boring' to 'what is the average weight of a bluebird?' Rarely did they make sense, but it always made her smile.

"Ah good, you're laughing. I've got the day off to a decent start."

"Why are you here anyway?" Ursula realised as soon as the words hit her ears how harsh she sounded. "I mean – well – it's great, and I wanted to see you. But I have my own pass."

"Oh, that won't work now," he dismissed. "I'm here for your IT orientation. It's all part of my new gig."

"I used to come here every day. Why would I need orientation?"

"It has been eight months," Rob reminded her.

Ursula's stomach flipped. The humiliation still prickled her cheeks.

"I didn't mean it like that," Rob reached out to touch her elbow. His brown eyes rippled briefly with sadness. Or maybe pity? It was gone before she could decide.

"I didn't mean 'orientation' in that way. They aren't putting you back to level 1. It's just that, while you were gone, we changed the security systems. Your card won't work because it's out of date." He gestured to the control panel and Ursula placed her card against the textured surface. A tiny red light glared back at her.

"See, you need me after all." Rob winked and waved his own pass. The doors opened smoothly, and the light turned green. "We'll just stop at my office so I can update your card, and then you are back to business as usual."

Ursula grimaced behind his back as they entered the elevator. Yet again, she had jumped to the worst possible conclusion. She needed to relax. She was back full time. Like any other, normal employee.

She moved her focus to the elevator doors, which had closed to reveal an oversized poster. The large white square was filled with the text "A BREATH OF FRESH AIR" in stylised green print with the 'I' replaced by a stalk of bamboo. Though she'd seen it before, she shook her head at the ridiculousness of it. It had always seemed odd that Swan was advertising at all, but it seemed worse somehow that her parent company put ads in their own building.

"What?" Rob asked.

"That." Ursula nodded at the ad and then had a rush of nerves. She glanced at the security camera in the corner of the elevator, hoping they couldn't hear her. They didn't seem like the kind of company that would fire her for a small comment.

To her relief, Rob laughed.

"Swan has been on the news non-stop since the government deal, but somehow we still need to advertise," he scoffed.

"Just what I was thinking," she agreed with a half-smile. The muscles in her shoulders relaxed. Of course, people could make fun of these ads. A company wouldn't bother to get upset over something like that. And Swan probably didn't bug the elevators, anyway.

"As if every employee here doesn't know the government made a massive deal with Ms Swaiteck for a million of the carbon converters," Rob continued, referring to the company's founder.

"Do we really need a million?" Ursula mused. The discreet tube, no thicker than Ursula's thumb, managed to perform the job of one hundred trees in transforming sunlight and carbon dioxide into a variety of good things, not least of which was oxygen. Painted light green and clumped like stalks of bamboo, they were already starting to crop up everywhere as the government rollout began, but a million seemed like far too many.

"I wouldn't trust the government to know what it needed," Rob replied. "I'm sure they had some think tank decide that was enough to make the population impressed. They will probably sell most of them to other countries for a huge profit."

Ursula didn't comment. It was better not to engage in any of Rob's conspiracies against the government, even ones that sounded completely true.

"But I will be excited when it's not Cygnet One getting all the credit," Rob admired. "When do you think will we see advertisements for Cygnet Seven?"

Swan had playfully named each of its subdivisions Cygnets. Cygnet One was the main base for the carbon converter production, and was always in the headlines. The others included the central offices, distribution, and a handful of labs, each quietly focused on developing their own inventions.

"Personally, I hope we don't get any attention for a long time. I don't think dream reading is going to be popular."

"You don't think everyone will queue up to have their dreams expertly analysed and scanned for radical new ideas or lost memories?"

"Unless things have come a long way while I've been gone, there isn't much to find." Ursula frowned. It had been too long since she had been at work. For all she knew the dreams were all vivid now. She might be too far behind to catch up.

"What's wrong?" Rob broke into her thoughts.

"Nothing," Ursula replied.

"You looked worried."

"It's just the first day back. It isn't going as smoothly as I hoped." Rather than explain, Ursula limply held up her card as the latest in the morning's setbacks.

"It's just a system update," Rob's voice softened. "It's really nothing personal."

Ursula nodded. Maybe if the morning had gone differently, she wouldn't be humiliated by a simple card update. But it all combined to surround her in a miasma of foreboding. First, that imaginary sound on her window – which her mind stubbornly imagined was a bird, making the moment oddly violent – then, her threatening image of a desert. The memory of it made the spot above her eyebrow ache. Involuntarily she lifted her fingers to the dull stabbing.

"It's been a long morning," Ursula found herself admitting. "You don't think it's a sign, do you? That I'm too far behind or I won't be able to come back?"

"Hey," Rob comforted her, his voice soft and hushed. He reached out but she stayed huddled in the corner of the elevator.

"It'll take a little time to get back into the swing of things," Rob offered, "but you are back. You're okay now. Just take it one thing at a time"

Only the words made her stomach sink. Was she okay? She had thought so only yesterday when she sat down to meditate. But that flash of desert could have been a backslide. It might be just the thing that would give her therapist a reason to send her home. Back to endless days in her flat with Herb. Or maybe they would just fire her. She couldn't expect Swan to keep paying for an employee who was – what? – hallucinating? Maybe she should tell Rob.

The elevator chimed, bringing her to her senses. She released her fists – vaguely aware of the bite her fingernails had left in her palm – and let Rob lead the way. Ursula couldn't remember if she had been to the IT department before. It made her realise how long it had been since she really spoke to him.

"I should have asked you before – how do you like being a department head?" she asked.

"It's going well. The hours are ridiculous because I'm on call 24/7, but I have so much access." His eyes glowed, turning the coffee brown to milk chocolate. "I'm responsible for anything related to security. It's like I am a magician's assistant finally learning all the tricks."

"Of course, you would love having all the passwords and secret files," Ursula grinned.

"Speaking of secrets –" Rob took her card and ran it through a machine on the table. "You have a therapy check-in with Jill today, don't you?

"Yes," Ursula hesitated. "Why?"

"I have a mystery – do you want to help me solve it?"

"A mystery?" Ursula took her card back, but kept her eyes on Rob.

"I don't want to tell you too much now because it might cloud your mind." He casually raised an eyebrow. Ursula wondered if he had been practising that move in the mirror. "Are you staying around for lunch?"

"I was going to go to the commissary. But what is going to cloud my mind?"

"I can't tell you anything until lunch. I need you to have an open mind." Rob paused expectantly.

Ursula bit her lip. She already had enough to deal with today. But Rob's little mission was likely to be fun. And she could do with a good distraction.

"So, are you up for it?" He sounded like an excited child.

"If you want me to say something to Jill, I don't think I have time. I have enough to talk to her about."

"You don't have to say anything to her, in fact, it will only take a few seconds."

"Is this another one of your conspiracies?" Ursula found herself asking. She wasn't entirely sure that was a bad thing. A little nonsense might help mellow her day.

"Of course not," Rob replied defensively. "This is more of a... puzzle. And I know you like puzzles. Besides, I have only ever been interested in conspiracies that rely on truth and facts."

"Like lizard men?"

"That was an article I thought you would find interesting. I didn't say I believed it. Necessarily." He crooked a smile. Ursula laughed.

"Alright, what is the mission?"

"All I need you to do is have a look around when you go to Jill's office, and let me know if you notice anything strange."

"What do you mean? Like an odd painting on the wall or a smell?"

"Okay, it needs to be something you can see, but no more hints. Take note of anything that strikes you as wrong, or unusual."

"How am I supposed to know what's unusual? I've been gone for months." Ursula paused, the reality of what he was asking finally sunk in. The thought made her hands itch.

"Wait, you think my therapist is hiding something?" she asked.

"Exactly."

***

The lab was two floors below the Mental Health floor. In the elevator – which thankfully opened this time – Ursula's eyes went immediately to the circle with a pale "6" inscribed in white, before pushing four. As the elevator slid into motion, she silently wished that the day had been arranged with therapy first. Between her meditation and Rob, the entire morning seemed angled towards seeing Jill. She didn't like going to the lab at the best of times.

The elevator doors swished open, revealing the open-plan space broken up a series of desks and tables. Why is everything always white, Ursula thought immediately. The walls were a blinding matt white that seemed to glow with light, spreading the white all over the room. The cold floor tiles were a perfect match, along with the desks and cabinets lining the walls. The only break in colour were for the machinery and various cables – most of them in silver and black. The starkness of it seemed more abrasive than the various shades of white, grey, and beige in her home. There the colours seemed restful. Here it was like a threat.

Or perhaps that was just because of the people in it.

"Finally," the booming feminine voice called from her right. Ursula bit her lip automatically, wondering if she had said her last thought aloud. The timing was just too perfect.

Ursula turned to see Trish push away from her table and stride over. The engineer hadn't changed either: her silken black hair was precisely pulled into a low ponytail with a part exactly in the middle, and her smooth skin managed to seem pore-less without makeup. Even her clothing didn't betray a wrinkle. She could have been computer generated, and gave the impression she wanted to be.

There was no welcoming smile. The thin line of Trish's lips stayed perfectly straight and her eyes narrowed as they locked onto her target. Despite being prepared for Trish's attitude, Ursula couldn't fight the feeling that she was shrinking where she stood. It was remarkable how someone shorter and slighter could loom over her.

"Hi Trish," Ursula managed to say.

"We have months of upgrades to get through," Trish deflected any social chat. "Most are tweaks but we have a new piece of kit to test as well, so we need to get going. You could have told us you were running late."

"I had to update my security card," Ursula offered.

"You didn't need to cut into my time to do that," Trish replied flatly.

Ursula had no idea what to say to that.

"Let's get started," Trish continued, leading the way to an empty station in the middle of the nearest row. The engineer glanced at the stool half-tucked into the table and offered no further comment.

Ursula sat down obediently, straightening her back. She used to do these updates every month, and yet somehow each time felt as uncertain and bemusing as the first.

Trish grabbed a pair of wire-embedded gloves from the table next to them, drawing Ursula's attention to the spread of awaiting equipment. Laid out in a series of overlapping piles were various sensors, visors, and other gear that looked like it would delight a gamer. There didn't seem to be any organisational thought to the arrangement. If anything, the kit was treated haphazardly, which put Ursula further on edge.

There was at least two hundred thousand pounds worth of work on that one table, surely someone in the lab should treat it with care?

But, looking around the various other stations, it appeared only Ursula thought of the equipment that way. When Ursula first joined Swan, she expected the labs to be neat and orderly with everything laid out like a museum. Instead, each station seemed strewn with odds and ends, piles of wires and electrical apparatuses. There was evidently a method to it, but not one that was known to anyone outside the lab. Ursula had come to think of it as stepping into the middle of an autopsy: the pieces might not be where you expected them, but someone was keeping tabs on all of it.

"Gloves first," Trish handed her two wire-embedded white haptic gloves. The thick white material was studded with sensors, and a series of black wires sprung from the palms like plastic hair. Ursula had the urge to ask why they chose white material when every electrical wire was coated in black.

"We've made the sensitivity better," Trish continued, as Ursula pressed her fingers to the ends of the gloves. "There should be more subtle variation in sensation now, and we think we have managed to integrate it better with the Medusa, so you don't have any extreme sensations like pain. But, without you, we can't really tell."

Trish gave Ursula a pointed look before she grabbed her hands and looked the gloves over carefully for any gaps in the fit. *As though I can't put gloves on,* Ursula thought to herself. Then another thought edged in.

"What do you mean you can't tell if they work without me?" Ursula asked. Her stomach giggled uncomfortably. "Hasn't anyone else been testing while I was gone?"

"No," she replied simply.

"Hold this." Trish shoved a plug into Ursula's hand. With the various wires and sensors, it was remarkably hard to grip.

"So, you have waited the entire time I was gone?" Ursula's breath became shallow.

"You knew that when you signed up," Trish replied as she shuffled through the remaining equipment on the table. "Beta tester Singular."

"But I've been gone for eight months," Ursula felt a heat blossom over her back and spread up her neck. It was true, when she was hired, the Medusa was in the first stage of testing, so only one subject was required. But she had assumed that over the past two years Swan had hired more people. Or, at least, replaced Ursula while she was on leave.

"No kidding," Trish rolled her eyes. "That's why we have eight months' worth of equipment waiting for you, so we don't have time to chit chat."

Trish snatched the wire back from Ursula's hand. Even under the layers of electronics and material she felt a sting. With a clunk, Trish stabbed the plug into a box on the table. The swift ferocity of it made Ursula flinch. Maybe Trish was thinking of stabbing her instead.

Trish then returned the table lifting out another piece of equipment to connect to the Medusa. Seeing it made Ursula relax slightly. You could see immediately why this machine was called the Medusa. Its metallic tentacles drooped off the central mesh body, which had the same flaccid appearance of a deflated balloon. When the cap was slipped onto the head of a dreamer the wires came to life, creating a cascade of electronic tresses that resembled the snake-haired mythical figure.

Ursula had only ever seen the Medusa on a person's head once, at her first day of training. They demonstrated the machine, explaining how each brainwave could be read individually and translated into computer code, allowing the dreams to be interpreted by a separate computer they called the Reader. Though she had only ever worked with the Reader, when Ursula settled in to watch a dream, she always thought of the Medusa. It offered her a sense of comfort, knowing the connection was ultimately always human.

Seeing it now, lying on the table in a heap, she felt a warm ripple of affection spread over her chest. Perhaps because it was the other half of her own Reader, tucked away back home in the secured closet. Or, perhaps, it was just a sign of how much she had missed work. The Medusa was the only reason her job existed. It recorded the waves and images of the Dreamers for her to analyse, filling her days, and giving meaning to her quiet life.

Trish unceremoniously jabbed at the Medusa – a sight that made Ursula flinch – before giving it a shake.

"Come on," Trish huffed. "Wake up."

Finally, the box that connected Ursula's gloves with the Medusa came to life with a green light. Ursula's mouth parted slightly. She'd never seen a direct hook-up between the Medusa and her equipment before. It felt strangely personal. Intimate.

"Right, we're hooked up," Trish declared. The awe clearly did not extend to the engineers who worked with the Medusa. Ursula watched silently as Trish moved to the nearby computer. With a few clicks, Ursula's fingers were overtaken by a sudden softness.

"Tell me what feel." Trish commanded.

"Uh…" Ursula closed her eyes and concentrated. The sensations that played on the pads of her fingertips were familiar but just out of reach. "It's a texture. Soft, supple, but not warm like a person or an animal. It must be a material. Wait – yes, I know it… um, velvet?"

"It'll be more accurate when you have your visor on," Trish commented, giving no sense of whether Ursula had been right.

"Now what do you feel?" Trish asked, her eyes glued to the monitor this time.

Ursula's hands grew warm, this time all along the fingers and over the pal of the hand. The heat began to undulate in waves, flickering at the edge of agony, then back to tolerable. Ursula turned her hand and found the heat shift across her wrist and around to the backs of her hands, indicating the heat was coming from a confined source in front of her.

"Fire," Ursula kept her answer short.

"That one didn't take too long," Trish commented before moving on to the next sensation. At least I know that one was right, Ursula thought.

They went through ten samples in the end, though Ursula wasn't certain how much more subtle the detail was than her previous gloves. It had been too long since she'd worn them. Yet, even before her absence, these sessions seemed like a test at which Ursula was merely guessing the answers. It was a relief when Trish gave a final nod.

"Well, that works," she commented as she banged one of the keys on the computer. The screen disappeared into black. "Take 'em off."

"Have you been updating the Medusa as well?" Ursula found herself asking as she gently pulled the tips of the glove away from her fingers.

"Why would we?" Trish asked. She was now beside Ursula and, having unplugged the gloves, she connected yet another device. Her interest was so mild that she didn't glance at Ursula while performing the simple task.

"Well, the Dreamers must have been giving you feedback while I was away," Ursula explained.

"What do you mean?"

"The people whose dreams I'm reading."

Ursula's stomach fluttered again. Had she said something wrong? Maybe she wasn't allowed to ask about the Dreamers. The fluttering in her stomach grew to a frisson. She turned that energy on the gloves, struggling to peel the material over her knuckles. It had somehow become too tight. Everything in the lab felt too tight.

Trish sighed, and put crossed her arms over her chest.

"Why would we know anything about the test subjects? I don't get any of their feedback, that's your department."

"But –" Ursula found the words disappearing before they reached her tongue. Of course, she didn't know who the Dreamers were. If it wasn't the lab, who did manage them? Who was collecting all this data if not the lab? She collected all her files from Trish.

"Come on," Trish groaned. "I meant it when I said we are pressed for time." The engineer yanked the glove from Ursula's left hand.

"Sssstt," Ursula sucked in a noisy hiss of air to keep from yowling.

Trish ignored her and flopped a pile of sensors onto Ursula's lap.

"Put these on, they're the same as the ones you have at home."

Ursula untangled the five main sensors in her lap, each shape unique to wear they fit on her body. As she placed the tab on her ankle, she realised that these original five hadn't changed. The haptic gloves and VR visors had become sleeker, slimmer, and more fashionable with testing, but the slim white sensor pads hadn't changed in any way. They were also placed in the same location, never varying over the months of testing. She had been doing it long enough to know each spot by touch.

The thought was comforting.

She placed the final pad against her forehead; her fingers laying the pad just at the edge of her left eyebrow and smoothing it along past the flattening of its arch.

It flashed suddenly with a burning Ursula knew was not being fed through the sensor. It was the memory of that morning. The piercing jab that she felt as the desert disappeared had been at the exact centre of her sensor.

Her hand froze, fingers hovering above the spot. The memory of it brought a faint ache to the surface again.

"This next one will be a little uncomfortable," Trish announced with a devilish smile. In her hand was what appeared to be another plug, but coated in a plastic membrane that implied it was not going to be inserted into anything electrical.

"We thought we needed to add a sense of smell. Tilt your head back so I can get a good angle on your nose."

Ursula was too disoriented to do anything but obey.

***

"Can you still feel any pain or aching?" Jill asked. The therapist leaned forward in her chair, her warm brown eyes wells of concern. She didn't reach out to the spot, but Ursula felt the warmth of her concern cover the feet between them.

Jill had always exuded that soothing wave of care. Or, she had for as long as Ursula could remember. The fragments of their early sessions – before the attacks – were hard to grasp onto, but Ursula vividly remembered her first impression. It must have been in that very office, but she couldn't remember the details of location or time. What Ursula remembered was Jill's round, welcoming face, her skin radiant and smooth as dark chocolate in the sunlight. That glow had emanated a deep feeling of welcome. Ursula didn't need to speak a word to know that she and Jill would get along. She couldn't remember feeling that comfort so quickly with anyone else, other than Rob.

Of course, that impression could have been coloured by everything that had happened since. Jill had been the one to help her through the last eight months, and the month or so before when the panic attacks came, a haze of nausea so great that she couldn't stand. When Jill finally knocked on the door, Ursula had to crawl to let her in, digging her fingers into the carpet and dragging her body across the flat. When she managed to wedge open the door, she looked up to see Jill's caramel eyes squinted with worry and nearly fainted.

Jill had taken over everything. She got Ursula upright, meditating, and arranged food deliveries until she could walk again. She checked in every day for the first three months. Eventually, Jill also performed the hypnosis that got Ursula back on her feet and back to work. And now she would have to help her through another strange experience.

The guilt made her bones feel hollow.

"No. The stabbing pain only happened when I was meditating. Right when the vision stopped – or maybe at the same time – it was only a second, I can't be sure," Ursula explained with an apologetic shrug.

"When I thought about it again in the lab, I realised it felt like the same spot. The ache then was probably just a memory."

"If the pain hasn't lingered, then I don't believe there is anything to worry about." Jill leaned back, and her round lips arched into a smile.

Ursula leaned back as well. Her shoulders fell with relief. It was going to be okay, she reassured herself, it wasn't a stroke or a tumour. Her mind had done more drastic things before, but she still had trouble telling the difference between physical pain and mental. But she trusted Jill to know.

"Knowing that this isn't a physical problem, do you have any thoughts on what you experienced this morning might have been?" Jill broke the silence gently. Her voice, even at full volume had the muted quality of a babbling stream.

"No. I thought maybe you would?" Ursula admitted.

"I have some thoughts. But first, I'd like to know if it reminded you of any of the physical symptoms you had before?" Jill asked.

Ursula noticed she did not specifically name either the panic attacks or EHS. She hated that term. Exploding Head Syndrome. It sounded like a cartoon, rather than the vivid experience of being woken up by the very real sensation of being smashed over the head with a sledgehammer. That horrid cracking sound, followed by the sensation of a physical blow to the head that split her skull in two. It had felt as real as breaking a leg, until she opened her eyes.

"Oh," Ursula realised aloud. "The sound. It was like the night terror: a pop or cracking just before the pain."

"And was the pain similar?" Jill asked.

"No," Ursula replied with a shake of her head. Disappointment curled like a snake into her stomach. For a moment she thought they were onto something.

"EHS was a crushing pain," she continued. "It felt like my skull had been cracked into pieces with a large smash. When I woke up it sort of lingered. But this morning felt like stabbing. It was sharp, and deep; I could practically feel it bore into me and then – snap – it was gone."

"That's interesting. I want you to consider that sudden shift carefully. And it's also worth noting that the sound was the same as what you experienced when you were sleeping," Jill commented.

Ursula tried to read what was going through the therapist's mind, but there was no hint in her calm, unlined face.

"Have you ever heard of a hypnic jerk?" Jill asked.

"When you are half-asleep and suddenly it's as though you're falling?"

"For most people it feels that way, but it doesn't have to," Jill explained. "Technically, it is a sudden contraction of your muscles just as you start to fall asleep. It causes the body to jerk or jump."

"But I didn't jump."

"No, but you did feel a quick jolting pain after a brief and fantastic image. It is not unlike falling asleep, seeing the beginning of a dream, and then the contraction of the muscles could startle you. Because of your history with being woken in the night, the pain and the sound might be an additional anxiety response you have. Or the pain could be a response to the muscles contracting."

"Maybe," Ursula hedged. She tried to remember the hypnic jerks she felt before, but most of her memories were still shredded tissue. This seemed – for no obvious reason she could explain – different.

"Let's think this through step by step," Jill offered. "How were you feeling just before you saw this image of the desert?"

"I was meditating," Ursula explained, "so I felt calm. Relaxed, I suppose. Do you still meditate?"

"Most days," Jill nodded.

"Do you know that feeling when you get into the rhythm of your breath and it's like your body sinks into the floor? Almost as if your muscles don't need to hold you up anymore, and you feel settled, no longer rushed with the day?"

"Yes, I believe I do," Jill nodded. "And then you had that flash of the desert?"

"Yes. It was without any warning, no feeling of dozing or sleep. Just bam –" Ursula clapped her hands together, "I was jerked away by the image and then blindsided by the pain."

"Isn't it interesting that you just said the desert 'jerked' you out of feeling relaxed, and the term is 'hypnic jerk'?"

"I guess."

"Occam's Razor, Ursula" Jill reminded her. The right side of her mouth quivered slightly, resisting a smile.

Ursula held back a sigh. Occam's Razor was becoming a theme of her therapy sessions. She couldn't remember the first time she heard of it. It was one of those ideas that must have permeated the universal consciousness, because it seemed like everyone referred to it at one time or another. Like the accepted wisdom of not going out in the cold when your hair is wet, or was a 'well known fact' that was also nonsense. You can't catch a cold from wet hair and, as Ursula often reminded Jill, Occam's Razor had been disproven countless times over many centuries.

"So, just because there are connections between meditation and sleep, I fell asleep?" Ursula could hear the edge in her voice, and felt a pull of guilt in her chest. Jill had gotten her through so much up until now. She shouldn't be so resistant.

"Why do you oppose the idea so much?" Jill asked.

"You know why: it's a disproven myth from the Medieval Era," Ursula replied.

"That doesn't mean that it can't also be helpful," Jill countered. "It helped us through the worst of your panic attacks."

Ursula wrinkled her forehead trying to remember. She knew Jill loved to bring up Occam's Razor, but she struggled to remember the specifics. It had been something about the hypnosis. Why they decided to do it. They couldn't change the environment she was in, so they had to change how she related to it.

"I guess so," Ursula shrugged. "And I can see the appeal of using this theory. It's tidy and simple; and it makes life seem simple and easy to deal with. But it is also a fantasy. It ignores the complexities of life and reality. In Occam's dream world – where his theory works – there would be no unsolvable murders, no falling in love with someone who wasn't ideal on paper, no 'opposites attract'."

Ursula found herself short of breath and paused. After regaining her composure, she added, "and, if I actually lived by Occam's Razor, I would be terrible at my job."

"I understand that Occam's Razor isn't the solution to everything in life," Jill acknowledged. "Dreams are complex and inconsistent because people are contradictory and surprising. But you can still apply Occam's Razor in situations where it is helpful. Like this one."

"We have several things that suggest this image of the desert was a dream: you were relaxed and meditating after a restless night; the sound is like the one you had when you were abruptly woken up; and the feeling of yanking or jerking sounds like muscles contracting as they do in a hypnic jerk. There is a clear line we can follow here."

"So, you think I fell asleep?" Ursula crossed her arms over her chest.

"I think you were *falling* asleep," Jill corrected her. "You said you were relaxed; your body and mind were calm and centred. It seems reasonable that you started to dream of the desert, and then your body jerked itself awake. Since you were sitting upright, your body probably reacted more dramatically so that you didn't fall over."

"And, if you don't mind me saying, there isn't a very compelling alternative. Can you offer any other explanation of what the desert might be if it's not a dream?"

Ursula's defiance wilted under the question. Her only alternative thought had been a stroke, and there was no evidence of that. Everything pointed to a dream. The very image of a desert seemed dreamlike. She had never seen a desert before, so why would she imagine one unless it was a dream. She brought the image to mind once more. The longer she considered it the more surreal the image appeared. No desert she had seen on film or photographs was that cliché, that barren and drained of colour.

"But what about –" Ursula paused. She had yet to mention that the pain had appeared in the exact spot where the Medusa sensor sat on her forehead. The idea of doing it made her extremities go cold. Making any connection between her mental state and her work seemed to lead in one direction: being fired.

When she first explained to Jill her morning, she'd claimed that the jabbing feeling of the olfactory sensor had brought the memory back. That seemed close enough to the truth without making the obvious connection between the Medusa and her frantic vision. Now she still felt the chill of danger at mentioning it. She had been back less than a day, there was no reason to risk her job over one small hiccup.

Besides, she reasoned, it really could just be a dream.

"Okay," Ursula agreed. "That does make the most sense."

Jill moved the session on to how Ursula was feeling being back at work, but for a moment it seemed to Ursula that her therapist hesitated. It might have been her imagination, but she could have sworn that Jill pressed her lips into a thin line and narrowed her eyes. As though knew that her patient was holding something back.

Jill

What are the ethics of lying to a patient?

The thought swirled around Jill's head as she rocked in her desk chair. She was fairly certain she had done the right thing by deflecting Ursula's vision of the desert toward the easy excuse of a dream; but right for whom? If this really was a one-time blip, what she'd done right by all of them. She'd certainly saved the company, and probably Ursula's health. There was no need to risk her spiralling again.

But if this was a sign of Ursula's memory coming back – of the hypnosis failing – then lying might make things worse for Ursula. Perhaps she should have warned her patient that the desert might come back. Maybe she should have hinted that Ursula needed to protect herself by not telling anyone else. But how could she do that without risking everything, or putting her patient in danger? If she overreacted now, there could be real consequences for Ursula's mental health.

A pang in her gut sent a well of tears toward Jill's eyes. She could feel them gathering behind her cheeks, fighting to get out. They came with the memory of Ursula writhing on the couch, screaming that she knew she was going to die.

Jill swallowed hard, forcing the tears away. *Yes*, she insisted to herself, *I did the right thing*. It was ethical to lie to save a life, at least this once.

But now what?

Jill flipped her mobile phone around in her hands. Each time the screen faced upward it briefly lit up, waving up at her and reminding her how much time had passed. The session ended twenty minutes ago, and she only had another ten before her next session. If she was going to call Mackenzie, she needed to do it now.

Her partner deserved to be warned, as the consequences were potentially too great for all of them. Yet, each time Jill unlocked her phone she paused, staring past the rows of icons to the photograph behind. It was just a selfie. Mackenzie and Jill smiling, huddled together against the rain with the Cornish coast stretching out behind them. Their faces were glistening with rain, and Mackenzie's auburn hair was whipping across her face in long, damp, twists. It was just a carefree holiday picture from five years ago.

Before everything happened.

Right from the start, Mackenzie had seen the dangers of it. She was visibly shaken from the start, but that grew into a deep unsettled anxiety. Only a week or so after learning about Ursula, Mackenzie had stopped sleeping through the night. One evening, Jill had woken to see the outline of her partner sitting stock still, her back rigid and upright, staring into the black of their bedroom.

When Jill turned on the light, the cotton sheets took on a tint of orange, mimicking the warmth of the August night. And yet, Mackenzie's arms had been covered in goosebumps.

"What if the government finds out?" Mackenzie had asked. Her voice was steady and level, at odds with the rigidity of her body. It reminded Jill of the shell-shock victims she'd learned about at university.

"How could they?" Jill had asked. Now she recognised her first reaction as denial, but at the time it had seemed farfetched. The government almost never paid attention to universities unless the MPs were looking for a pleasant way to retire. That seemed like something out of a movie, or at the very least out of America.

Mackenzie only continued to stare.

"You said no one saw Ursula arrive," Jill continued, trying to buoy Mackenzie with her voice. "We know no one is looking for her. And you said the lab was empty, and the security man at the desk didn't look up when the two of you left. So, there's nothing to raise suspicion. And as far as her living here, no one pays attention to their neighbours anymore. If they noticed at all, they probably think we have a guest."

"Maybe no one is suspicious now," Mackenzie replied solemnly, "but when the carbon converter goes public, I am going to be under a lot of scrutiny. The government, energy companies, the newspapers; they will start looking into me. The NCA might investigate simply because of the implications of the converter. Everything will be under a microscope: my research, my work history, but also my personal life."

That was when Jill realised the true risk. It hadn't come as a shock, more an inevitable rising of the tide. She remembered her body felt heavier with the acknowledgement. Once they were under scrutiny, it wouldn't take long to come across Ursula – certainly not if she was still living with them. Even if they happened on the connection accidentally, it would raise questions they could not answer.

"People will be looking at you, but if Ursula isn't living with us anymore, there's no real connection," Jill reasoned. "And going forward we can just claim she is a former patient. No one will be looking into my background, and doctor-patient confidentiality can act as a shield."

"I'm not sure that's enough," Mackenzie sighed. "Maybe the government wouldn't investigate a casual friend, but energy companies aren't known for playing by the rules. Nor are the press. What happens if they get suspicious of the friendship, or just decide to investigate anyone close to us."

They both fell into silence. Outside their flat, a group of people were calling to one another in booming voices. Students, Jill thought. She remembered feeling a pang of jealousy that life was so simple at that age. They weren't yet responsible for themselves, let alone anyone else.

"What would happen if they did get hold of her?" Jill asked hesitantly.

"It depends on who gets their hands on her. The worst would be the government." Mackenzie wrapped Jill's icy hand in her own.

"They would likely start with questioning, and possibly drugging. If they believe she knew more than she does, then torture wouldn't be out of the question."

"How could they justify that?" Jill felt tears prickle in her eyes. "She is a person."

"Not to them. To them Ursula would be a prize. They would get what they wanted out of her however they could."

"Ursula must know that too," Jill realised. "That must be why she came to you."

"I'm not sure why she came to me," Mackenzie confessed.

Jill saw a cloud pass over her partner's eyes. None of them were prepared for this, but the extra weight on Mackenzie seemed brutally unfair. Bringing a secret like this to one person might make sense in the abstract, but in practice, Jill could see it begin to crush Mackenzie. It was going to change her, if it hadn't already.

"Maybe we should make this public? Tell everyone who Ursula is and what happened?" Jill heard the nerves in her own voice. She struggled to steady them.

"Could you imagine the fallout?" Mackenzie finally came to life, her eyes frenzied and her hands shaking.

"At least half of the people won't believe us. Those that do would politicise the situation, trying to use her to their advantage. And Ursula would certainly be taken. If not by our government, then another one. Or worse, they could kill her. More than one company would want her dead."

"I'm sorry, you're right," Jill stoked Mackenzie's arms, trying to sooth the panic she'd created. She chided herself internally for being so foolish. There was a reason Ursula came to Mackenzie, and at least part of it was privacy.

"She may not be around much longer," Jill offered. It was their best hope; and at the time, it still seemed possible.

"If she was going to disappear, it needed to happen weeks ago. We must accept that all three of us could be in danger. We need a plan"

Over the course of that long night, Jill and Mackenzie carefully arranged to hide Ursula under the layers of camouflage that a large corporation like Swan could offer. Thanks to the tech companies of Silicon Valley, no one raised an eyebrow and companies essentially owning people's lives. Swan just had to copy the enclosed worlds of Google or Apple into their own HR policies and watch as Ursula disappeared into a pool of employees living off the 'perks' of their new job.

With each carefully added layer to the plan, Jill could see Mackenzie trying to distance herself from Ursula. It seemed reasonable and necessary for Ursula's protection, but Jill sensed there was something else motivating the change. When Ursula went to work as an official employee, Mackenzie had insisted she keep a distance. There were no more dinners together. When they crossed paths outside her office, Mackenzie would physically stiffen.

When Ursula had her breakdown, Mackenzie still wouldn't see her. Maybe it was too dangerous, but surely a boss could check in on an ill employee? Jill had argued from every imaginable angle in her effort to force Mackenzie to reconnect, but the wedge between them held firm. She treated Ursula like she was radioactive. And it had forced a distance between Jill and Mackenzie as well, as Jill was forced to deal with the situation on her own. She didn't resent it – she wanted to help Ursula – but she was hurt that she couldn't rely on her partner.

And with the hypnosis blocking out most of Ursula's memory, she felt like she was holding the secret on her own. Somewhere along the line, she had stopped updating Mackenzie on Ursula's progress. The only positive comment Mackenzie made was when Jill first suggested hypnosis.

"It's a good plan," she had said, her voice cold and official. "Smart. If Ursula doesn't know the truth, who else could find out?"

"That's not why I'm doing it," Jill had to remind her partner. "I am trying to help Ursula, so she can have a real life, here and now."

A rogue tear broke free with the pain of the memory and rolled down Jill's cheek. She glanced nervously down at her mobile, watching as the droplet disturbed the black reflective surface.

Without wiping it away, Jill slipped the phone back into her purse. For now, she would wait and see.

Ursula

She had forgotten to look for anything strange in Jill's office. Seeing Rob across the commissary, the thought brought her to a halt. Ursula waved and smiled, but inside her body went hollow.

She searched back through the past hour straining to remember what she'd seen in the therapist's office. It wasn't overly decorative. There was the usual sofa, which always looked clean but worn in. The walls were mostly bare, painted a dusty muted blue, like the ocean under a cloudy sky. The bookcase was filled with the usual mix of books and decorative – but noticeably therapeutic – objects, like soft toys and stress balls.

Only two things in the room ever felt out of place: the blinking silver camera used to record each session, and Jill's chair. Rather than a chair to match the sofa, Jill used a desk chair specially designed for back support. Sleek and grey but minimal, it was the only thing in the room that fit in with Swan's laboratories. Everything else looked as though it was designed to be comforting and plain.

But she hadn't been looking very closely. If something had changed, or something new was on the bookcase she probably wouldn't have noticed. Her shoulders hunched inward, protecting her from the sinking feeling of guilt. She would have to come clean, and hope Rob wasn't relying on her too much.

"So, how was it?" Rob asked as she joined him at the table. He'd chosen a table in the corner, far from any of the other diners.

"Fine," Ursula avoided Rob's eyes.

"Don't tell me you forgot."

"Rob, I'm sorry." Ursula bit her lip. "For what it's worth, nothing stood out to me, but I didn't specifically have a look around. I had something else on my mind, and it just took over the whole session."

"Is everything okay?"

Ursula hesitated. She didn't want her entire day to be preoccupied with a brief image of desert. She looked up at Rob – his forehead crinkled, and his eyes drooped in worry – and gave in. Recounting the morning to Rob, she emphasised how calm and assuring Jill had been. She was also careful not to mention the pain that came with her dream; it would only upset him.

"I'm sure Jill's right. It's just a dream. Something like that happened to me last Saturday. The team took me for drinks to celebrate the promotion. The next day, I was so hungover that when I did a standing meditation, I must have started to fall asleep. One minute I was looking at the poster on my wall, the next my arms were flying out and my head was tumbling to the floor."

"You probably tipped because you were hungover."

"It certainly didn't help," Rob admitted. "But I am quite sure I drifted off. It goes to show that anyone can fall asleep while meditating."

"I'm not sure this is the same thing. You didn't see anything." Ursula shrugged but also felt a smile creep to her face. It was comforting that this kind of thing could happen without a complicated mental health history.

"Well, you are conditioned to notice dreams," Rob pointed out. "You probably just remember the start of your dream, whereas I never remember anything that happens when I sleep." Have you ever been to a desert before?" Rob interjected.

"You're lucky," Ursula scowled into her sandwich. Life was unfair. Rob had never even had a nightmare. "Anyway, it wasn't much of a dream; it was just a dry yellowing desert with some sand in the wind. I doubt that's worth my brain remembering."

"Well, dreams have hidden meanings – or so your job tells us. Maybe the desert is symbolic of your barren social life." Rob grinned, his cheeks puffing up like a chipmunk.

"Charming," Ursula reprimanded with a playful glare. "Or, maybe I dream of the desert because my best friend won't come and visit, leaving me completely alone?"

"Hey, I text. I'm a good friend. Besides, you are the one who failed in your important mission to help me out," Rob reminded her.

"Sorry," Ursula offered again. "For what it's worth, I doubt Jill has anything in her office other than work."

"Well now the world may never know," Rob replied, his voice taking on the tone of a documentary filmmaker.

"Alright, I will remember next time. What am I supposed to be looking for anyway? You promised you would tell me."

"I guess I did. But, before I say anything, I need you to promise that what I say is completely secret." Rob leaned forward conspiratorially.

"I can't imagine they would trust you with anything confidential," Ursula gave him her best incredulous stare.

"They have no choice," Rob retorted. "I am one of the bosses now. And just for that I might not tell you the classified things I am getting up to."

"Are you allowed to tell me?" Ursula asked.

"No, not officially," Rob replied.

Ursula couldn't detect any sign of teasing in his face or voice.

"They make us sign non-disclosure agreements almost every day," Rob explained, "but, realistically, they expect us to tell someone."

Ursula shook her head.

"Nope, I don't want to know anything that gets me fired," she insisted.

"Seriously, it's built into the system," Rob explained. "Everyone knows that having a secret is impossible to keep;

and the more important the secret, the harder it is to resist telling someone. You might be able to hold it in for a while, but at some point, you would just burst. And that could happen in front of a competitor, or a journalist. So, they unofficially let us confide in a trusted colleague within the company – like you – to get the information off our mind while putting nothing at risk."

"And I won't tell and get you fired?"

"Of course not. I am, literally, your only friend." Rob grinned.

"And I have such good taste," Ursula took a large bite of her sandwich.

"So? Can I trust you?"

"All right, your secret is safe with me," Ursula gave in. "Why were you snooping around Six?"

"I wasn't snooping. In fact, I wasn't even on the therapy floor. My work was purely within regulation: I was going over the electrical maps to maximise the efficiency and minimise the wiring in the building... Never mind, I can see your eyes glaze over."

Rob laughed. He wasn't wrong.

"The point is that on the schematics there was an extra wiring panel on one of the walls for a security lock. One for a door inside the therapist's office that is not in any other room on the floor."

"So what?" Ursula asked. "There are fingerprint locks all over the building."

"Just wait." Rob lowered his voice, despite the nearest person being two tables away.

"When I looked closer, I realised the lock was wired separately from the rest of the electrics on the floor. It's not even wired into the main alarm – it has its own dedicated patch."

Rob paused, his eyes wide and glittering with drama. Ursula took another bite of her sandwich.

"I don't get it," she admitted. "A closet has an alarm and it's not hooked up to the door alarms; but it doesn't need to be. It's just a lock for that person's closet."

"Shh –" Rob chided. "I told you already – this is a secret. Can't you keep your voice down?"

"Fine," Ursula barely whispered. "What makes you so suspicious about this lock?"

"Weren't you listening?" Rob's words strained against his own excitement. "It's not patched in. It's entirely private. I realised immediately that something was strange, so I looked at the building schematics – this keypad isn't indicated on any of them. And there's no sign on the blueprints of a room, or a closet, or even a wall safe. Whatever that lock is for isn't on any of the plans..."

"That *is* strange," Ursula admitted.

"More than strange," Rob pressed.

"Wait and this was in Jill's office?" Ursula's sandwich was suddenly hard to swallow.

"That's the weirdest part. I can't tell. I went back to the electrical schematics and realised that because the entire floor is symmetrical, there was no way to tell which direction was which on the plan. And because the room – or safe, or whatever – isn't on the blueprints, all I can tell is that it's on a wall between two central offices. It could be either office, on either the east or west wall. There are four options, and Jill's office is one of them."

"Okay," Ursula tried to reason through the swamp of information Rob had put before her.

"But that is still not very suspicious. Like you said, it could be a wall safe. That's not a strange thing for someone to have. And it could just be a mistake that the electrical plans aren't clear."

"And that the blueprints don't have any sign of the hidden room?"

"Would schematics have a safe on them anyway? I doubt it." Ursula replied in a firm, but gentle voice. She didn't want to dismiss her friend entirely, but she always had a niggling doubt when he came up with one of his conspiracy theories.

"Urgh," Rob groaned and rolled his eyes in a single pointed move. "I said it could be a safe. But the lock is just as likely a room, especially with the space between the two walls. It's an entirely hidden room – why would they need that on the therapists' floor? Why would they need a safe for that matter? The entire area is incredibly well protected, with key cards to enter the hall, a security alarm, and locks on every room. No other room needs a super-secret hidden space with its own unique locking system and alarm. It's suspicious."

"I see what you mean," Ursula hesitated. "But you have to admit, you do tend to get overly excited about things that turn out not to matter."

"I can't believe you are comparing an unofficial security door to the FONO App," Rob threw his hands in the air.

Ursula had, indeed, been referring to Rob's international online campaign demanding to know why an App had changed its logo from green to purple.

"You took a week off work to picket outside their offices," Ursula reminded him. "The CEO had to hold a press conference."

"It worked," Rob reminded her, "I got an answer."

"Yes," Ursula nodded, "they admitted that they changed their logo to a purple background so it would stand out more among the other Apps."

"And I never said it was anything more than that."

"You thought it was a sign they were a Ponzi scheme. One of your message boards was trying to hack the user data to prove they had bank account information."

"That was someone else's idea; a rogue faction of the movement," Rob dismissed. "Anyway, this is not the same thing, because we know something is fishy. We have an actual hidden door that is not on any record or known by anyone and is even hidden on the building documentation."

"Except you easily found it," Ursula reminded him.

"And," Rob persisted, "when I tried to go to the therapy floor to investigate, security guards showed up and escorted me out."

"They have guards on the therapy floor?" Ursula had never seen one before.

"No, it was one of the regular entry people. He must have come up from the lobby."

"Why would a security guard come up six floors to remove you? For all they know, you were going to your therapy session?"

Ursula tried to imagine how she would have felt if a guard stopped her on the way to today's session. She didn't feel hungry anymore.

"They knew because of this thing," Rob replied, waving his ID card. "Remember your little nemesis from this morning? You've been away too long if you forgot our schedule is linked to these."

"Right," Ursula squeezed her eyes shut, pushing away the frustrations of her morning.

"But, as you were saying, there is no reason for him to sprint six floors to stop me," Rob continued.

"And you think he did that because they were worried you would find a door behind one of the locked rooms that they don't even know you know about?" Ursula almost laughed.

"Ignoring your cynicism, the million-pound question is: what is behind that door?" Rob leaned back in his chair with a satisfied smile and a glint in his eye.

"Do you have a theory?" Ursula asked. She might as well let him say what he wanted to say and get the theory out into the universe. It might keep him from doing anything stupid.

"My first thought was that it could be a solitary confinement room."

Ursula snorted.

She couldn't imagine any company being stupid enough to try and confine their employees, let alone in a windowless hidden room that no one could have access to. It was about as likely as an evil lair.

"Okay, that is a bit over the top," Rob waved the suggestion away, "but it is a therapy office; and the door seemed like it had a bad energy about it."

"You can tell from a blueprint that a door has bad energy?"

"Sometimes you have to trust your gut," Rob replied.

Ursula's chest panged with envy. She hadn't been able to trust her own gut instinct in months.

"What has a bad energy?"

Ursula's shoulders jumped at the cheery voice from behind. She whipped around to be confronted with Sage, the striking engineer who shaved half of her head, somehow making the long, thick, black locks on the other side seem more lustrous. She dropped her tray of sushi on the table and looked between the two of them expectantly.

Ursula glanced back at Rob. How much had Sage heard? What did Rob expect Ursula to say? How much and how little of this secret could get them in trouble? Perhaps she should lie.

"I'm trying to convince Ursula to do some spying for me." Rob replied.

Ursula stared at him. How could he dump this on her?

"You can go up those offices any time you want, why would you need to recruit Ursula?" Sage asked, seemingly unaware of any tension.

"I found a hidden door." Rob relayed the entire secret, leaving nothing out. Ursula was surprised by her own disappointment. Perhaps Rob had told everyone.

"You're an idiot," Sage replied bluntly. Without warning, she turned to Ursula.

"Tell him he's an idiot," she commanded.

Ursula's mouth opened, but all she could mutter was an indistinct "Uh..." Her thoughts struggled forward as they waded through the thick glue of her mind.

"Where do you think therapists keep all their patient tapes and files?" Sage turned back to Rob, leaving Ursula adrift in her confusion. "On bookshelves every patient can flip through? Stored on a hard drive in their desk for anyone to stumble on? No. They keep it in a safe like any normal person."

Rob's smile faded into a thin line.

"But –" Ursula's voice had finally, sheepishly, returned, "in that case, every office should have one. Every therapist would keep their own files private. Rob only knows about one door for certain. If it's the only one, it wouldn't be for patient files."

"Not necessarily," Sage countered smoothly. "The head of the department probably keeps all the files to make sure they stay secure and on location."

Ursula found her words failing her again. She ground her teeth in frustration but couldn't come up with any counter argument.

"Ugh. Fine, that is one possible answer. Why do you have to be so logical and sensible?" Rob moaned.

"Well, I have a PhD and work with some of the most advanced technology on the planet, while you are paid to not get electrocuted," Sage stuck out her tongue playfully.

The gesture made Ursula bristle.

"That still wouldn't explain why I wasn't allowed to access the lock, though," Rob added hopefully.

Ursula smiled.

"He's right. As an IT head he should have a right to check on any of the security doors, even if only to make sure it was working properly. And, I've been thinking, why would they need physical storage?" She added. "We haven't used DVDs in months; I think Jill stores all her sessions on her laptop."

"Yes," Rob's smile widened, and he jabbed his fork in Sage's direction. "Plus, the door was normal size, as if it opened into a closet or a room. You don't need that kind of storage for some DVDs and a backup drive or two."

"You are overthinking it," Sage shook her head. "The simplest solution is probably the right one."

Ursula wondered for a moment if Sage also had Jill as a therapist. She hoped not.

"Which therapist's office was it?" Sage asked.

"I don't know, actually," Rob replied, wiggling his eyebrows. He went on to explain the strange lack of information that meant the hidden room could be any of the offices.

"But whichever room it's in," he insisted, "I am certain there is more to that door than patient files."

***

Ursula slid the glistening crisper drawer into the lowest level of her refrigerator. The entire interior now smelled vaguely of lemon, and the shelves were, at last, tidy. The jars of half-filled condiments that had long passed expiration were now emptied and drying beside the sink. She closed the door and looked at her watch. It was only 9am.

"Damn." She breathed. After a beat she glanced to the nearby doorway. "Sorry Herb, I know you don't like cursing."

What plant did? She thought to herself, silently. Somehow, she had managed to do everything on her list. After so many months stuck at home, the only things left were those rare niggling chores that never seem quite worth the time or effort. It wasn't a thorough list, but she thought it would at least get her to lunch.

"Well, there's nothing left to do now," she admitted, and walked to the meditation room. She offered Herb a smile. His leaves were plump and happy with water from the day before, and the sun was hitting him in a pleasant column of yellow light.

At least his day is off to a good start, Ursula thought. Not that mine isn't, she added quickly.

Settling into her usual position on the carpet, Ursula looked out to the ocean. The sky was a pale blue, stretched thick enough to make it almost seem white. The sapphire shadow of the ocean stood out below, cutting a clean horizon line as far as she could see. Usually, the sight would send Ursula's chest upward, and unlock the kinks living behind her shoulder blades. Today, they remained hunched, even after a few slow shoulder rolls.

She closed her eyes to block out the sight and tried to steer her mind towards her breath. With her eyes closed, the twists of energy writhing through her body amplified. With each breath of air, her ribs spread, fighting against a slithering around her heart. Her mind was just as unsettled, jumping from thought to thought in a series of overlapping, punishing waves. It flitted from the refrigerator, to Jill, to the conversation she'd had with Rob and Sage; at one point she caught herself wondering what she wanted for dinner. They were mundane thoughts, but ones she was normally able to push aside.

Ursula shook her entire body and grunted in frustration.

Maybe she should lie down?

She settled herself back, struggling to find a comfortable angle for her arms and legs. Finally, palms up, her shoulder slightly crooked, it was comfortable enough. She breathed in.

The carpet itched.

"Arrrggghh." She sat up roughly, throwing her hands over her knees, and looked at Herb.

The plant was seated on its perch: peaceful, patient, and calm.

Like she should be.

Ursula forced a huff of breath through her nose like a dragon and stalked out of the room. She snatched her phone off the bedside table and returned, falling into her spot with a painful thud. She ignored the singing soreness of her hip, and flipped through the audio files until she found the right meditation. She jabbed it on, faintly aware of how disappointing it was not to have a button that clicked.

A tinkling of chimes faded into the low, steady rhythm of a woman's voice, guiding her through the meditation. Her thoughts were no less chaotic, but the voice forced her to return to her breath each time. By the final chime, her head ached with the effort of concentrating on her breathing.

She opened her eyes and felt a soft tug beneath her ribs.

Nothing had happened.

The pressure under her skull loosened, but her chest remained hollow.

Ursula walked over to Herb and brushed a fleck of shining dust from one of his buds.

"Jill was right. I must have fallen asleep." Saying it out loud didn't fill the persistent vacancy of her chest. If anything, it made it grow heavy.

I shouldn't feel this way, she thought. *Nothing bad happened. I should be happy.*

Jill's voice faintly floated to mind: Nothing good comes from 'should'. Ursula breathed out so that her lips puffed and sputtered. Maybe what she was feeling was relief?

"Well, I've wasted enough of my morning." She patted the bookshelf as a goodbye to Herb and crossed the living room.

Seeing the keypad, she smiled.

Over the months at home, she had forced herself not to open the closet. It just reminded her of the work she wasn't doing and the life that had started to slip away. There had been some days when she was tempted, coming up to the wall repeatedly or occasionally starting to type in the passcode. She had forced herself only to open it once a month, to clean off the material and make sure the computer was still functioning. It became harder each time to close the door behind her, but she had. Finally, she could use the Reader again.

The keypad light glowed green and the door opened with a sigh. The air was stale and heavy with the scent of plastic, but the room was beautiful. The chair, fitted to the contours of her body, was a welcoming, comfortable centrepiece. Seated upon it was the headset, reflecting the sunlight in two winking eyes.

"Hello," she replied to the Reader's winking greeting.

With an unconscious familiarity, Ursula unravelled each sensor of the Reader and stuck them to the usual spots. She ignored the twinge of nerves as she placed the pad on her forehead, and turned instead to wrapping the cuffs around her ankles. The wires inside the material were still worn around the jut of her ankles, making it easy to fit into place. Next, she slipped on the new gloves. Away from the lab, it became obvious that the material was stiff. In time it, too, would feel like a second skin.

At the nose sensor, Ursula paused. Her nostrils tingled remembering the uncomfortable jabbing when Trish inserted it the day before. Delicately she slipped it into her nose. There was a pressure as it grazed against the cartilage, but otherwise it settled into place smoothly. Ursula scowled. She knew that Trish had made it more painful than necessary – although breathing through one nostril would still take some getting used to.

With that thought, Ursula settled herself into the chair, its material warm and smooth against her legs. She took a deep breath and her shoulders slipped down a notch. She was back at work and back in control. It felt right.

She scrolled through the laptop giddily wondering where she should begin. Perhaps a short dream to start with to ease herself back into things. She clicked on the shortest dream in her queue, slipped on the headset, and leaned back into her chair.

This, she reminded herself, *is my anchor*. She took a slow, measured breath in and released it in a lengthy hiss. Her mind and body sunk into the chair and the moment. With a click of the button by her ear, the headset burst with light.

It lasted two seconds. Images fluttered before her like pages of a book; a single chord stretched in her ears; then she was plunged back into the dark.

"Hmm," Ursula hummed thoughtfully, trying to solidify her mind around any first impressions. Most of her dreams were too short to be read at average speed, but she always liked to play it through once at speed, just in case something sprung immediately to mind. After all, this was how people dreamed.

She clicked the recorder on inside the helmet and listed the serial number of the dream and the length. "First impression has no strong emotion. I'll go through next at $1/60^{th}$ speed."

She adjusted the playback rate and ran the dream again.

The sound was essentially the same, but now the images became clearer. The visuals of the dream began with a muddled background of green and yellow. She knew from experience that the seemingly abstract design was made up of a mesh of translucent pictures layered over one another. As the dream progressed, new images fell on top of this backdrop – one after another – adding to the web-like haze below. Like a translucent flipbook, some fresh images seemed to move or bleed into the next one, but she recognised some of them already.

She made a voice note of the images that seemed clearest: a face, a building, a lake, a fish, a crowd, a maze, a sheet of words. In the great pile, the most recent image was the most distinct, but she could also see the outlines and distinctive features of images two or three deep. There was something soothing about watching as the images slowly melted into the semi-opaque mess below.

"Final assessment, frame by frame."

Ursula diligently noted down each of the forty-six images that appeared over the course the dream. None of them seemed connected, but she reminded herself that it wasn't her place to assume. Any details that reappeared – blonde hair, the arch of a nose that matched the slant of a lake – were remarked on as well.

Going over the list, she was struck how different the static vision of her desert dream had been. The details were clear and crisp in her vision, whereas on the Reader every image from the first to the last was muddy and blurred, melting into the mesh spiderweb of a background.

She wondered if it was worth making a note to see if the Medusa was muddling the dream experience. Then she thought of the scowl Trish would make when she heard.

I'll stick to analysing, Ursula decided.

The sound was next. At the slower speed the note lowered an octave, but remained a single reverberating chord. It had no obvious relationship with the images, but the sensors on her body emitted a comforting warmth at the sound of it. Ursula noted it and then ran through the musical scales on her computer until she found the chord – B flat.

Now let's try something a bit more interesting, she thought as she went through the list once again. She sorted the files by time and then scrolled straight to the bottom.

Longer dreams were usually more detailed, giving her plenty to sift through. Her eyes rested on the bottom two dreams, each over two minutes.

Perfect.

At that length they would be episodic dreams; the kind that felt like a genuine experience. She selected the longer of the two dreams and brought down her visor.

Her stomach churned. It spat up a wave of heat that smothered her entire body from the inside. Her head ached and pitched. The darkness was moving all around her.

Oh, Ursula realised. Seasickness. The familiar flush of nausea meant the dreamer was moving. She had once trained her mind to accept the sensations of movement when her body was still; she would have to relearn that particular skill.

She focused herself on the movement, following the sway of each leg and the rhythm of weight moving with the dreamer's steps as they walked. When she could feel the weight of each footfall clearly through the sensor pads, the queasiness passed.

The screen of the headset faded in with the ghostly outline of an enclosed space. She could sense the confines of the hallway before they solidified in her vision. Though it was wider than the halls of the Cygnet building, the space felt claustrophobic. On impulse, Ursula tried to reach out to touch the wall, but of course, the dream body was unresponsive, pushing steadily ahead.

The sound of the footsteps arrived in her ears – or had they always been there? – tapping in time with the movement of her feet. Ursula strained to pick up any other sound, but there was nothing. Not a breath, nor an echo to soften the clack of each individual step, which was marking the time with the inhuman regularity of a metronome.

Three.

Four.

Five.

The hallway extended before her, white walls stretching out indefinitely into a hazy eternity. Instinctively, Ursula tilted her own neck, straining against the stubbornly singular perspective of her headset. But the image didn't change. Locked dead centre onto the vanishing point, the perspective didn't blink or jostle in response to the movement of invisible body below.

A new sensation grew along her arms and legs; a magnetic pull drawing her entire body forward in an intractable tug. A thought overcame her, either from her own mind or the dreamer, that the hallway was now in control. It was driving her forward in an eternal march to nothing, ending only when her body collapsed.

Somewhere far away, Ursula felt her throat contract. The gulp was like a memory, only faintly reaching into the world she now shared with the dreamer. She tried to grasp onto the reality of her own body when something snapped into vision.

The distant stretch of the corridor began to warp, curling around the shape of a door. It was as white as the walls with a single, rectangular golden handle just visible in the distance. Her hands went cold – or perhaps that was the dreamer's hands? They itched to reach the handle but were also aware of a clinging foreboding.

Her legs began to feel heavy, though they kept their stolid pace. The hallway drew her on. Her limbs became leaden, and her chest sunk with weight, urgently trying to anchor her to the spot. But the steps clacked mockingly back, noting the constant progress, no matter how her body tried to stop it. Her skin seemed to swim down her skeleton, dragging to the floor under the heft of gravity, but she kept moving forward.

A silent scream wailed in the distance, perhaps from her own body? It grew... It was a woman's voice. She couldn't remember if it was her own. The scream morphed into a moan of frustration, grunting, and calling at her, but never quite breaking into the sound of those footsteps. It must be her, the real her. Somewhere back in her body, in her own mind, she wanted to break away. To scream, to burst into the dream and claw at the wall, tearing her out of its clutches.

Finally, unexpectedly, the door was only four steps away. Then three. Then two. The sound and the movement stopped.

The moaning was gone. Silence sunk into every corner of the hall. The weight in her arms lifted.

The door hovered for an unforgiving moment before a tingle raced up her arm. She watched the foreign limb reach out in front of her, crossing the gap between her body and the handle. The metal was cool in her palm as her fingers wrapped around it. Her gaze sifted, focusing briefly on the reflection of her arm in the yellow surface. She caught a glimpse of the arm, enrobed in a pale blue. Her hand tightened around the handle and pulled open the door.

A flash of yellow swarmed her vision – a whisp of sand swirling into the dry air, a blinding wall of heat. The desert appeared before her again, expanding in all directions, as wide and bleached as the face of Mars. She opened her mouth to take in the desert air.

The image collapsed with a bright stab into her forehead. Her insides lurched, as though a fishing line had hooked onto her organs and slammed them against the internal walls of her body. Her lungs compressed. She gasped for air, but nothing was there. She might as well have been floating ten feet under water. Her vision went black.

Her legs lunged forward. With a sharp twinge, her head jerked backwards from the nose, like a fish on a hook. Her neck snapped back with a wrenching ache.

Collapsed in the chair, Ursula yanked her helmet off. She cried out as the olfactory sensor scraped along the inside of her nose, wasting the last of the air in her shrivelled lungs. Her computer, desk, and array of wires appeared before her. A warm drop of blood trickled from her nose. She gulped fresh air. Her right nostril burned. And then her body began shaking.

Ursula took another deep breath and shoved her convulsing hands under her thighs. She took another breath and could hear the air drag around her teeth. And another, as she wrapped herself into a ball, squeezing her legs so tight the muscles couldn't move.

It had to be the same desert, Ursula thought, her head buried in her knees. She recognised the flat landscape with three cracks over the surface and the puff of dry wind causing the dust to kick up in a dramatic swirl.

As her mind settled, she felt the heat radiating off her body. She pulled off her gloves and unstrapped her ankles, yanking the sensors off at the roots. The equipment fell into a pile on the floor and her lap. For a moment she thought of the table in the lab. She wanted to laugh – or cry.

There was only one way to tell if it was the same desert, Ursula realised. She swept the sensors in her lap to the floor and jammed on her VR helmet. As it grazed the spot above her left eyebrow, it sent an aching pulse through her skull. She gripped onto the arms of the chair with as much force as she could manage and replayed the dream from the beginning.

Re-watching it with only the visuals warped Ursula's perspective from the start. Rather than walking down the hall it looked as if the dreamer was still and the walls on either side slid past. It reminded her of a stationary bike where no matter how fast you pedalled you didn't move. There was also no sense of dread. If anything, she was bored watching a plain white hallway slither slowly past. It took most of the two minutes before the door finally came into view with an anticlimactic smallness.

The hand reached out. The dreamer looked at their arm reflected in the handle, and then pulled. The door opened into blackness. The dream ended.

Ursula chewed the inside of her cheeks irritably.

She played the dream again, on half speed.

And then a third time.

Then she went over the last two seconds frame by frame. But it wasn't there. No yellow, no desert, not even a hint of sand.

She wanted to scream.

Instead, she took off her helmet and placed it carefully beside the computer. She sat back in the chair and stared at the blank ceiling, a ray of white sunlight slicing it in two. In the silence of the room, she was forced to admit it. There was no longer any doubt. The desert had not come from the Medusa. And it was not a dream.

Mackenzie

Mackenzie looked out the window of Jill's office onto the rainy, crowded streets below. The spread of umbrellas transformed each person into a near circle. From four stories up they appeared like cells moving through the bloodstream of the city, jostling, weaving, and pushing through the veining streets in a moderate flow.

There are too many people, she thought, not for the first time. She could feel the muscles around her eyes twist into an involuntary grimace. More people meant less space, less food, less water, more struggle. It meant more resources were needed to keep them from becoming too aware of the mass slip into poverty and hunger. Maybe it was inevitable. Maybe the carbon converter just gave humanity a permission slip to keep on moving ahead as they were. Or allowed them to become more destructive.

A lump thickened in her throat. If that was true, what was the point? Was it worth the years in research, the hours up late at night, the struggles of the past five years building Swan, fighting off other companies? She didn't know anymore. If things were only getting worse, then none of it mattered. Not even Ursula.

Mackenzie rubbed the spot between her eyebrows. There was no use going down this road. The past could not be changed, but the present needed to be dealt with. Whatever the future held.

"Do you think it's the Medusa?" Mackenzie asked. She adjusted her vision to take in the reflection of the glass. Jill was still at her desk, her head resting in her hand. It was hard to see her partner this way; her heart ached less looking over the existential doom of the outside world.

"Causing her visions?" Jill's voice seemed to float, the words coming into being without being directed at anyone.

"Yes." Mackenzie answered shortly. She cleared her throat to steady her voice. One of them needed to stay in control. "Dreams are known to impact long-term memory; and we still don't entirely understand how the Medusa or its Reader work. It might serve to improve memory, reversing the hypnosis."

"I doubt it. The first vision happened more than eight months after she was off the machine," Jill reminded her. "She was meditating."

"I mean that working with the Medusa might be making the situation worse." Mackenzie clarified, turning back to Jill. She could keep her face neutral now.

"Maybe the first little blip of memory would have gone away on its own, but then she straps herself into the Reader, and it naturally reinforces the memory. Improved memory could be an unexpected side effect. Equally, maybe the device isn't compatible with a mind subjected to hypnosis."

Mackenzie resisted the urge to point out she hadn't wanted to use the machine in the first place. She wanted to focus on the carbon converter, something she understood inside and out. Diving into people's dreams had never been an interest. It was only after the hypnosis, that Mackenzie reconsidered. Ursula needed a job, and they could use this opportunity to figure out how the machine worked safely on someone who had used it before.

"Ursula said it was safe," Jill insisted. Her voice was firm, but she was also scratching her wrist. The one nervous habit she never managed to master.

"Technically, it is safe. It isn't harming her by improving her memory. On anyone else that would be a serious benefit." Mackenzie held back a sigh. "It's just not in this one case."

"Maybe," Jill shrugged. "But the first memory had nothing to do with the Medusa. I don't want to take her off the machine unless we are sure it's affecting her."

"I don't see that there are any other options. And we need to stop this now, before anything else happens." Mackenzie sat on the desk and loomed down at her partner. It was a corporate move, but she needed Jill to see the light. Ursula was a risk now. They needed to act like it.

"You are overlooking the obvious," Jill deflated, her shoulders slumping further. "What if I did it wrong?"

"Jill –" Mackenzie reached out to her partner. At Mackenzie's touch, Jill leapt out of her chair.

"I've never done hypnosis like this. Very few people ever have. Blocking out traumatic memories is not a recommended clinical solution, and it's not like I could ask for expert help. I did my best, but it wasn't enough."

Jill's olive skin flushed with red. Her face welled up under the strain of tears.

"You did your best, no one could have done more," Mackenzie soothed. She wrapped her arms around Jill, holding her close enough to feel the heave of each stifled sob.

Her heart ached. She wished she knew what to say or do to take the burden from her partner, to help her let go. Every night she watched Jill replay Ursula's taped sessions, checking to be certain her patient was doing well. The books stacked by her bed were all related to hypnosis or memory loss in patients. And Jill always woke before the alarm on days when Ursula was scheduled for a session. No one could have been more devoted to a patient, and no therapist needed to be.

"You did exactly what you were supposed to, and we know it worked," Mackenzie reminded her. "She hasn't had a single blip for eight months. Almost nine. Maybe if she never came back to work, it would have gone on indefinitely. It isn't you; it must be something about Swan that triggered her."

"No," Jill said, her voice eerily calm. She pushed herself out of Mackenzie's arms. The red drained from her face and she pressed her lips together thoughtfully.

"No, it isn't work. You made a good point: it's been months. The hypnosis could be wearing off with time."

"I'm not sure about that," Mackenzie offered quietly. She didn't want to make things worse.

"Hypnosis to block memories is not a hard science, and it's not consistent," Jill persisted. She was becoming more animated and the worried lines in her face cleared. "Maybe it needs regular topping up? Like you said it was working fine until recently."

"Until she came back to work," Mackenzie pressed.

"No. Before work," Jill emphasised the two words as she might a small child. "Yes, it was the same day, but she was doing her usual morning routine. And she used to come to the Swan offices weekly for therapy. It can't have been showing up that did it. It must be the hypnosis."

Mackenzie tilted her head from side to side, sloshing about the idea. There wasn't any obvious flaw.

"I suppose it's possible."

"It's worth trying, at least," Jill insisted.

"Okay," Mackenzie replied slowly. "But I wonder if it might be worth having someone else come in to do it."

"Are you mad?"

"She's lucky to have someone who cares as much as you do," Mackenzie hurriedly explained, "but therapists aren't supposed to get too personal. It's already affecting your life."

"But you're right; maybe that's part of the problem," Jill put her head in her hands, muffling her final words.

Mackenzie stopped herself from saying anything more. Jill's dedication had more than once led to an argument between them, and she didn't need to relive it now, when the stakes were so high.

"I can't believe you are bringing this up again," Jill shook her head. The disappointment radiated from her, causing Mackenzie to bristle.

"Would it be impossible?" Mackenzie's voice cracked under the weight of emotion. "Especially now that she can't remember the past; do you really need to be the one working with her?"

"Ursula is remembering something. That's why we're here," Jill reminded her vehemently. "And hypnosis to block memories is most effective if you know what those memories are. Would you like to bring a stranger to this situation?"

Mackenzie looked away. Of course, no one else could manage Ursula, the risks were too great – for all of them.

"I just think you are asking too much of yourself." Mackenzie forced her voice to stay low and steady, but kept her eyes on the corner of the desk. "If something is going wrong with Ursula, you can't help her if you are run down."

"I'm not asking more of myself than you are." Jill's voice bit.

"I have not done anything close to what you are doing," Mackenzie scowled. "You put yourself at risk every single session. Once a month you look her in the face and talk to her and keep any hint of the truth back. I don't even speak with her. I am doing nothing compared to what you put yourself through."

"We don't need to have this discussion again." Exhaustion crept into Jill's voice. "Ursula is struggling, and we are all at risk. Adding guilt – and your jealousy – won't help the situation."

Mackenzie bridled. She looked up, ready to defend herself, and stopped when she saw Jill's eyes.

"The simplest, and most obvious, answer is that hypnosis is failing," Jill continued. "When she comes in tomorrow for the emergency session, I'll do the full process again. Then, going forward we will reinforce it every six months to keep well ahead of this happening again."

"Okay," Mackenzie nodded. What else was there to say?

She looked across to her partner. The room seemed larger, now; the distance between them uncrossable. She swallowed the first inkling of tears.

"We have to take care of her, Kenzie," Jill said. Her voice was small and laced with sadness, but it built a bridge between them.

"I know we do." Mackenzie wrapped her arms around Jill. This time she could feel her partner's warmth.

A smile crept on her face. Hugging at the office felt pleasantly sneaky. Of all the secrets that were hidden in Swan, their relationship was by far the most wonderful. Silently, she willed everything to be alright. She wished that Ursula would continue peacefully on the path they set out for her, and that there would be no need to confront the past. All three of them needed to move forward.

Her thoughts flitted to the long-delayed hope that she and Jill could have a child. There were so many plans that they had once had. The business had happened, but not the family, nor the holidays, or hobbies, or new friends. Mackenzie promised herself that they would take their life off hold – once they could be sure Ursula wouldn't remember anything.

Ursula

Immediately after the hypnosis, Ursula noticed her body felt lighter. Her limbs felt like they were floating free of the clutch of gravity. When she speared her salad with a fork, it seemed possible her arm would pass her mouth entirely and float up to the commissary ceiling.

"Is this the same hypnosis you had before?" Rob asked.

"Yeah, because it's still panic attacks," Ursula explained. "I'm not completely sure I understood Jill's explanation perfectly but essentially the first vision of the desert was the start of a dream. But I was still worried about it when I had a panic attack on the Medusa. And that's why the image came up again, looking exactly the same, perfectly clear."

"Is that a bit like PTSD? People having flashbacks."

"I didn't ask," Ursula admitted "but I think she did say it was like a flashback."

"And you feel better now?"

"I feel great. It's actually kind of surreal. I'm not sure when I felt this good."

"I always thought I should do hypnosis," Rob mused, tapping his fork against his chin. "They say it can help with almost anything."

"And what problems do you have, exactly?" Ursula smirked.

"I have a problem with you remembering to look around for a secret door," Rob wrinkled his nose at her.

"Aha!" Ursula beamed. "I actually did remember this time."

"Aren't your eyes closed when you get hypnotised?" Rob raised an eyebrow laden with scepticism.

"Yes, but I wasn't being hypnotised the entire time," Ursula jabbed at her salad in mock frustration.

"So?"

"I'm not really sure you need to know. I mean if you can afford to tease me about it, it must not be that important after all."

"You're being cruel! You really must be feeling better," Rob laughed. "Actually, I have an update: I can confirm that only one room on the entire Mental Health floor has a hidden door."

"How did you find that out?" Ursula was surprised by her own curiosity.

"Uh-uh." Rob shook his head. "You tell me first: door or no door?"

"Sorry, no."

"How hard did you look?"

"I looked," Ursula insisted defensively. "You would have been proud: after we finished, I said I needed to stretch. I used that chance to have a proper look at each wall. There wasn't a seem or shadow on any of them. And most of them were blocked by furniture or bookcases, so there was only one or two places wide enough to be a door."

"The door is pretty well hidden," Rob reminded her. "But I will temporarily cross Dr Annan off the list."

Rob pulled out his phone and crossed Jill's name off a list. Ursula glanced at the row of ten names. It seemed too many for one building.

"I notice Dr Wheatley is also crossed off the list," Ursula pointed to the name of Rob's therapist.

"Yes," he smiled. "That is how I know not every room has a hidden door."

Rob motioned for Ursula to lean forward so he could whisper.

"Yesterday, I arranged an emergency session, pretending that I had a terrible nightmare and I had wet the bed," he began.

"Seriously?" Ursula twisted her mouth in disgust.

"Well, he wouldn't have arranged an immediate appointment unless it was serious," Rob waved a dismissive hand. "Anyway, once I was in the room, I started re-enacting the fake dream:

punching the walls, pushing and thrashing, sometimes rolling around on the floor."

"What was this dream?" Ursula laughed. The image of Rob wrestling with thin air was too much.

"I had a fight with a grizzly bear right there in his office. Genius, right?" Rob beamed with pride. "It meant I could go anywhere in his room I needed to; and the rolling got me right at carpet level. I was very thorough. There is no way he has a hidden keypad or a camouflaged door."

"I would have liked to see that," Ursula giggled.

"Now, I just need an excuse to go to the eight other rooms."

"Not all eight, surely? Didn't you say it was in the middle of the hall? You can cross off anyone on the ends."

"You genius!" Rob grabbed her hand and gave it a squeeze. He then turned to the phone and began ticking off half of the remaining names.

Ursula blushed. It was strange being touched so suddenly; but it wasn't unpleasant.

She hadn't heard from him since that conversation. It had been almost two weeks, but maybe Rob had been too busy to do more sneaking around.

Her own week had grown better and better. The day after the session, she was on edge, but went through her normal routine and five dreams without an episode. That night she'd managed to sleep a full eight hours. She couldn't remember when that had last happened.

The next few days ran on their usual rhythm. Meditation fluctuated day to day but she always left it feeling more grounded. She could feel some of her confidence using the Reader return as well. She was getting through as many as eight dreams a day, and finished every night feeling productive. She would be able to make up for lost time in a matter of weeks. Herb seemed to join in the excitement, as the first little buds of a flower began to appear at the centre of his leaves.

Ursula also felt brave enough to watch the other episodic dream on her list. The Dreamer was flying. Ursula wasn't fond of heights, but every sensor on her body was sending her tingles of joy and rushes of endorphins. She couldn't stop smiling, even when recording her voice notes. It seemed like fate that she chose that dream on a Friday; it was the perfect way to end the week.

And now that the weekend had come, it finally felt like a break. She toyed with the idea of going for a hike, but really all she wanted was to lay out on the beach. It was early enough in spring that the days were mild, but the crowds wouldn't be piling in on the trains and with their cars. For a few more weeks, she could count on the peace of the ocean.

She got up early enough to get a tea while the café was quiet and made her way down to her favourite slip of beach. The sun was already high enough to turn the sand white and the ocean teal. In the distance a couple were walking along the surf, a spaniel splashing at their feet and attacking the waves.

Ursula found a curve in the dunes to shelter her from the wind and made a well in the sand with her cup. She settled down in the quiet corner, her legs stretched out, pointing towards the waves. Under the midday sun, the surface of the beach was warm to the touch, sending a pleasant flush through the back of her legs. She dug her fingers under the sand as she leaned back and turned her face to the sky. Her eyelids glowed a golden yellow as the light poured over her. She smiled. The thrum of the ocean and the heat of the sun; what more perfect moment could there be?

Her entire body felt light and airy, without the usual buzz coursing through her chest. Maybe they should do hypnosis every month, she mused. The steady crush of the waves filled her ears and washed over her body. A seagull was squabbling in the distance. She gave herself over to it. Watching the yellow of her eyelids speckle as the clouds moved.

Her vision shifted. The yellow bleached out into the expanse of desert.

It was happening again, but this time she felt as though she were watching it, calmly, but curiously. Her vision scanned the flat, jaundiced horizon. The sand over the cracked surface was dirty and dry, easily shifted by the gust of wind into the familiar swirl. She took in the expanse for a fraction of a heartbeat before her vision shifted down. Against the sandy backdrop appeared a sleek black hand, palm facing upward. From that angle she knew it must be her own, though it looked unearthly and black as a shadow. It must have been a glove, but the strange matt cloth showed no lines or seams. If it had not moved, she would have believed it was a shape cut out of the horizon. The fingers flexed causing a cascade of blue to flicker and dance along the surface of the material that stretched up her arm; the sunlight catching on thousands of tiny scales that made up the surreal material.

Ursula gasped. Her eyes flew open but found only the curling caps of the waves as they tumbled down into the beach.

What was that? Her thoughts scattered in a thousand directions, none coming close to a response.

She reached up to her forehead, pressing her fingers against a sudden ache. It was the same spot. It had been the same desert. And now there was more of it.

Jill

"You have to take her off the machine." Mackenzie insisted. Her words sharpened as they hit the cold stone surfaces of the kitchen, piercing Jill's ears.

She grimaced. She had just replayed her voicemail to Mackenzie and her partner barely took a moment to think before responding. Jill had expected to discuss the Medusa again, but now it sounded like a command.

"Taking her off the Medusa would be cutting her off from her job yet again. She needs something to give her days meaning, like all of us," Jill countered. "And she was fine for most of the week."

"And then she had another, longer memory with more details than before. You heard what she said: she saw the heat suit."

"Only for a moment," Jill's voice wavered. She couldn't deny the memories were becoming stronger.

"Why are you so resistant to the idea it could be the Medusa?" Mackenzie asked, her jaw jutting out. "It seems like the most logical option."

Jill ground her teeth. For most of their lives together they were naturally on the same page; but when it came to Ursula, Mackenzie refused to listen.

"There are a lot of reasons," Jill insisted. "For one, if the Medusa was interfering with the hypnosis, I would have seen signs of this earlier."

"Maybe, but maybe not," Mackenzie remarked. The tone of her partner's voice stabbed at Jill's heart.

"Two," she took a step towards Mackenzie, trying to push back the wall of stubbornness with her body.

"Only one of her memories came back while she was working with the Reader. The other two happened when she was at peace – meditating and sitting on a beach."

"So, you think it's meditation now? She meditated every day for eight months without any of this." Mackenzie crossed her arms over her chest. Her voice had moved up an octave. It sounded childish.

"No," Jill clenched her hands into fists beside her face and threw them down again, forcing her excess anger at the floor. "But I am saying the connection isn't the Medusa."

"Then what is it?" Mackenzie demanded. "Because if it's meditation, or just inevitability, then we have no way out of this."

The fire drained from Jill with a wash of cold. Her fingers felt like ice. No way out. The words sunk into her chest, dragging hope with them.

"What if there isn't?" she asked. Her voice no longer sounded like her own.

"Don't think like that," Mackenzie dropped her hands to her side. Her face softened and her shoulders curled forward. She looked vulnerable. Beautiful.

And yet, at the same time, so very far away.

"You are doing something here completely without precedent," Mackenzie continued. "There were bound to be challenges and uncertainties. This is stressful, but that doesn't make it impossible."

Jill felt exhausted. She no longer had the energy to speak, and what would be the point? In her gut, she knew it wasn't the Medusa. But Mackenzie was right too; if it wasn't the machine, there wasn't anything else they could do. There would be no solution, no options, no answer. It put them back at square one with nearly a year wasted. And if Ursula's memory came back what could that mean?

The image came again of Ursula wailing and writhing on her couch. That, she reminded herself, might be the best outcome. One slip and everything could collapse. They would lose Swan immediately; and Ursula too. She might be killed. And deep in her soul Jill knew they would take Mackenzie too. These might be the last free days of her life.

"Let's just think this through logically," Mackenzie suggested softly. "Like an experiment: trial and error. We tried bolstering the hypnosis – and it may have helped slightly – but it wasn't the cure. The next best guess is the Medusa. It may not be perfect, but we should try it anyway – if only to eliminate it as a trigger."

"Okay," Jill agreed. Suddenly her bones felt heavy in her body. "We can take her off the Reader; but I want to stop meditation as well. I think we've got to consider meditation, given her latest vision."

"Thank you," Mackenzie reached out, but Jill backed away. For the first time she could remember, she didn't want to be touched.

"In the meantime," Mackenzie continued, putting her hands back at her sides "I'll see where else we might be able to put her. If this works, we can just slot her into another Cygnet and move forward."

"I don't think you realise how hard this will be for her," Jill found herself speaking. "She had been desperate to come back to work and we are basically telling her she's still mentally unfit."

"We'll call it a holiday. Tell her this is the department's fault; that we are worried the machinery isn't safe. It's basically true, and it shifts the blame to us."

"Mm," Jill made a noise just to let Mackenzie know she'd heard. None of this sounded like a promising idea; but she had nothing else to offer.

"We're doing this for her, Jill. I am doing everything I can!"

"Right," Jill replied in a hollow voice. She noticed Mackenzie flinch. Before her partner could argue, Jill returned to the matter at hand.

"I'll call her now for a phone session. It's better not to bring her back to work. How long is this holiday? Two weeks?"

"A month would give her more time," Mackenzie remarked, returning her emotion behind the mask of calm. Like an automaton, Jill thought.

"I don't want to scare her into feeling this is permanent," Jill pressed her lips together.

"Okay, then we'll try two weeks," Mackenzie agreed. Now they both sounded detached.

Jill remained still, not sure how to remove herself from the room when their conversation still seemed to hang in the air. What could her partner possibly expect her to say?

"Hopefully," Mackenzie ventured, "with this, the memories will stop on their own and we can place her somewhere else in the company."

"Maybe," murmured Jill. "Maybe not." She picked up her mobile from the countertop and left for the privacy of her office.

Ursula

The reverberation of the glass resounded like something dropped into water. It was the same noise she'd heard on her first day back. And she was once again watering Herb.

On reflex, her eyes went to the glass. She forced her attention back on the tiny succulent. The pebbles surrounding it growing mahogany as they soaked in the water.

Phommm. The sound came again.

She put down the watering cup and looked squarely at the glass. At first, she saw nothing – the window cleanly framing the view of the village and the ocean beyond – but then she noticed a fleck of white. It wasn't any larger than a fleck of paint.

Ursula went for a closer look. There were two marks, each close together. It was hard to tell what they might be. She reached her fingers out and rubbed the area, but the dots didn't budge. She squinted.

The specks weren't a solid white, they were opaque, changing colour with the movement of the sky beyond. She realised that they must be small dents in the glass; divots on the outside barely cracking the surface.

"Strange," she said to no one.

A streak of black hurled at her face. She stumbled backwards, nearly losing her balance.

Buooommmm. The black ball bounded against the glass. It recoiled a few inches and steadied into a hover. It was a bird. The smooth black wings resembled a Raven or a Jackdaw, but it was far too small to be one. And the beak was bright orange. With a flutter of wings, it rushed at her again.

Her sharp intake of breath drowned out the sound of the body slamming into the window. Before she could think, a second bird joined in. Black as night, but this one with a streak of grey over its wings. She stared at it for a beat when the next drum drew her attention to the first bird again.

Then a third hit.

And a fourth.

Next a cluster appeared, colliding into one end while the black bird struck at another. The beats against the window were too many for her to follow. Each time adding more beats, like a racing heart.

Soon it was five at once. Clouds of black and grey slamming the glass with enough force that she could feel the vibrations in the carpet beneath her feet. The sound seemed to call out to every other creature in the area. Soon it was a swarm. A sea of birds in black, grey, blue, and even flashes of red ricocheting off the glass and returning for more. They drilled relentlessly at her, slamming their fragile bodies into the glass. The thrum, like the pelting of rain, grew faster and louder, drowning the room.

With the sound of popping ice, a web of cracks splintered outwards in one corner of the glass. The room grew dark as the cloud of birds descended, blocking the sun. Ursula tried to gasp, but her throat felt full of wool.

The beating grew louder, vibrating the glass with a squeal. She could no longer tell apart the birds that were flying towards her and those that had been thrown back by the glass. The only hint that they were even moving were the twinkles of light that sprung up between the bodies as they moved.

Another crack splintered across the surface, a handful of tendrils snaking over the full length of the glass.

Help me! Please, please, help! Silent screams behind her eyes cluttered like the piled cars of a derailed train. The strangled words echoed in her head, building in ferocity, but never breaking through. She tried to trash, to lunge, to leap, to move her body in any small way. She needed to get out. The glass was going to break.

She fought to get the words out, her heart pounding inside her ears, her mind on fire. Help me! Someone! Anyone! Please! –

"Help." The word finally broke through, in a whisper.

She was in her room. It was dark. The walls of the room were navy blue in the dimness of reflected moonlight. Her breathing was steady, as was her body.

She sat up sharply, hearing her breath cut into the silence. The duvet fell away from her body, abandoning her bare arms to the shock of the cool night air. She flexed her fingers and wriggled her toes. They responded immediately to her command. A gurgle of relief bubbled in her chest. Quickly replaced by a squeezing sickness in her stomach. A forceful burp broke from her mouth, but she managed to keep down the familiar wave of sickness that came with her night terrors.

It had been months since her last nightmare. Why was this happening again?

***

"It's not the Medusa. With the nightmares coming back, I think I'm losing my mind again," Ursula's voice quivered. Just saying the words aloud seemed dangerous.

"You aren't," Rob insisted.

As he shifted beside her, Ursula could feel grains of sand flowing away from him and running over her fingers. Usually the sensation would be welcome, but now it felt like the beach was trying to bury her alive. She shook the sand from her hands and placed them in her lap.

"It sounds like they are taking you off the Reader for your safety, so maybe the nightmare is also a side effect of the machine," Rob replied. His voice was soft with reassurance.

"This is the risk of testing new equipment," he continued. "Sometimes it has unexpected side effects. I bet that in a matter of days things will feel normal again. When they do, you can tell Jill and they will move you to testing something else."

"I know it's not the Reader," Ursula insisted. "I've only been back one week, that's too fast for this kind of effect. And the desert showed up after months off work, remember?"

"Didn't you have to test the equipment once a month while you were on leave?" Rob reminded her.

"Yes, but that was just running through one dream to make sure the sensors were functioning; it wasn't like a full day's work; and it wasn't every day."

"Maybe once a month is enough," Rob suggested. "I mean if the head of the company – the woman who invented this machine – thinks it's enough; then it probably is. For all we know the side effects could be much worse. Maybe it caused your anxiety attacks? I bet this paid holiday is Mrs Swaiteck covering her ass."

"I guess," Ursula sighed. She didn't want to think about the 'holiday'. From the way Jill said it, she would bet anything that this was a gentle way of the company telling Ursula they thought she needed more mental health leave. The thought made her scowl.

"You have a tendency to think the worst of things," Rob reminded her. "But I really think it'll be okay. Once you are off the machine for a few days –"

"It *isn't* coming from the machine!" Ursula nearly yelled. She immediately pressed her lips together to swallow her frustration. "Please, will you just believe me for five minutes?"

Rob's eyes drooped. After a beat, he looked away, focusing on the ocean.

"What have you been doing behind my back?"

Ursula bit her lip.

"I know you," Rob continued, "You wouldn't be this certain without evidence."

"You have hunches and gut feelings," Ursula looked away, trying to focus on the hazy line marking the sea from the sky.

"But you don't."

The silence stretched for long enough that Ursula could feel guilt clawing its way up her stomach.

"I looked into all the archives of dreams collected by the Medusa," she finally admitted. "There isn't a dessert in any of those dreams."

"That's a breach of security," Rob smirked. "You realise they could fire you."

"If they think it's the Medusa, they'll have to fire me anyway. I can't do my job if the machine is making me see things. Making me lose my –" the word stuck in her throat.

"You aren't losing your mind," Rob insisted. He placed a hand to Ursula's shoulder.

"And I'm not upset, I'm impressed. Breaking into backfiles is my kind of thing, but I never thought I'd see you do it."

Ursula looked up to see her friend grinning. She lifted the left side of her mouth. It was kind of ironic.

"The point is that I know the desert vision can't have originated from the Reader or the Dreamers," Ursula continued more confidently. "If it was the machine, then the desert would have been buried in one of the dreams and the visions would be my mind struggling to integrate the dreamer's unconscious. That's how Jill explained it. But there wasn't a single desert image in the entire file. I've put in the hours, I know."

"I hate to say this, Ursula, but that doesn't necessarily mean anything. If it's subliminal or subconscious, then it wouldn't necessarily show up in the dream. Say you have a dreamer who lives in the desert; that information might be buried in dreams and brainwaves as symbols, or some other thing that doesn't show up on your sensors. The brain is a complicated thing."

Ursula sighed. She looked up at the sky hoping she would see rain clouds forming, ready to pour down over her and drown her in misery. The sky was mockingly blue and clear.

"You're right, I don't know if there is another connection between the dreamers and the desert," she admitted slowly. *But...*

"You have the IT backfiles and access to any information stored on Swan's computers, right?" Ursula asked suddenly.

"Technically, I could access it..." he spoke carefully.

"That means you could find out about my dreamers. Who they are, where they are from. If they lived in, say, a desert, or if they travelled to the Sudan regularly."

"It's a blind study," Rob shook his head. "That information would be too personal for Swan to ask. And if they did, it would be an invasion of privacy for me to find out."

"But not really. I'm not trying to find out who they are so I can talk to them or sell them something. If just one of them lives near a desert or works in a desert, I can know it's the machine, and that I am not going crazy. And with a solid link, we might be able to pinpoint what's wrong with the Medusa and I could go back to work." The words tumbled out in a waterfall of emotion. She could feel her cheeks get hot.

"Would you want someone looking into your files? Or worse, using your name or address to try and stalk you online and find out where you lived?"

"It's ethically awful," Ursula looked away. "But I am desperate. I'm certain it isn't the Medusa, but no one will listen to me. Not even you."

"This won't necessarily prove anything. Who knows why people dream about things? It could be some desert they saw in a movie," Rob's voice was getting higher.

"Okay, you're right it's not the way to prove this isn't the Reader, but it might give me something to hang onto," Ursula's mind raced. This felt like the only answer.

"What if one of them does live in a desert, or maybe works as some engineer in the Sudan. If just one of the dreamers really does have a connection to the desert, it would prove me wrong, but then I would know. I could now that there really was a reason to think the Medusa was giving me these visions."

"This goes against everything I believe in. You know this. I think companies take too much interest in our personal data already." Rob's neck started to go red.

Ursula realised she had never seen him angry before. A pit grew in her stomach, but she couldn't give up. If he investigated the files and saw no one lived outside of desert-less Britain, he would realise she was right.

"Please," Ursula begged, a large tear falling to the ground. "You don't have to tell me anything specific. You could just say 'yes' or 'no'. They do or don't have some connection to the desert."

Rob wriggled his toes in the sand, causing an earthquake in the tiny mountains above his feet. The tiny grains scattered in a thousand directions, tiny rivers of destruction, collapsing to reveal the edge of his toes.

"I'm sorry Ursula, but I can't do this," Rob insisted. His voice was steady and his eyes remained on the ocean, away from her. "It's unethical, and illegal, and it could cost me my job."

He was right. Ursula felt a cold wave of guilt add to the growing pain in her chest. She tried to apologise, but her throat choked with tears. All that came out was a blubbering murmur.

"But," he continued, looking back at her. "I will see if there is some authorised – legal – way we can find out." I don't agree with Swan keeping data on blind studies, but if they have it, there may be an official route to accessing the information."

"Thank you," Ursula gurgled through the tears and lunged at him.

It was the first time they had ever hugged. He felt warm and smelled of talcum powder.

She thought of that hug again as she settled down to bed. Her head still ached with the intensity of crying hours before, but it was easier to bear now, with the hope of what he might find. She fell asleep certain Rob would find the answer.

The next day, that feeling of warmth vanished. Ursula woke feeling empty and cold. She wished she felt sick, or tired, or anything she could use to distract herself. With nothing better to do, she made tea and walked into the meditation room.

"Jill said not to meditate," she reminded Herb. "So, I guess I'm not going to spend as much time with you today."

Herb's buds appeared to droop under the news.

"So here I am, not meditating. And not working. Not. Doing. Anything."

Ursula looked out onto the ocean. The waves were choppy that morning, tussling curves of white foam thrown against one another. She glanced back at her plant companion.

Herb was silent.

The room was silent.

She thought of her dream and her stomach clenched. Maybe silence was a good thing? At least that was an event. It might have been a nightmare, but it was something happening; something to prove the world was alive. That she was alive. That life was interesting.

"It's just like before: nothing to do," she commented, thinking of her months on leave. "Well, not quite the same. I spent months with nothing to do but meditate, and now I have less to do. It's like solitary confinement. Isn't that supposed to make you insane?"

A band of sunlight shifted to highlight Herb.

"Okay I'm not alone," Ursula admitted to him. "But you aren't chatty, are you? And you have to admit it's frustrating. You and I sitting at home with nothing to do. Again."

With her eyes, she followed the beam of light that surrounded Herb down to the floor and over her foot.

"Oh, you are actually doing something aren't you?" The thought curdled in her mind. "You gather the sun and the air and make it breathable and make yourself sugar and that is your entire life. You don't have a day off. You don't need one. I, on the other hand, have been forced to take two weeks! And that is somehow supposed to drive me less mad – make me less angry, less ridiculously useless and frustrated and – grrraahhhh!"

Ursula flung the tea mug across the room. With a thud it fell to the carpet just shy of the wall. The yellow-green of the tea sloshed over the carpet like an invisible incontinent dog.

"Damn it," Ursula sighed. She closed her eyes and took a breath.

"It's not your fault," she mumbled, to herself and to Herb, as she went to get a towel from the kitchen.

After several dabs she'd soaked up the worst of it, but there was still a faint yellow outline on the carpet. She looked from the towel to the carpet. Except for the stain they were a matching white. It suddenly struck her that most of her room was the same vacant white. Each strand of carpet was effectively blank, and they gathered to create a mass of nothing. Her floor was a flat, dull, sanitary, vacancy.

"Look at this place" she puffed at Herb. "Why didn't you tell me, it's so empty."

She looked around her, taking in the bland void. The carpet was a greying white - bleached in places and stained in others – but effectively an extension of the dingy white walls. The pillow she used as an occasional bolster was an anonymous beige. Her pale oak bookcase offered the only break in the sanatorium chic. Crowned by the pale green and dusty pink of her succulent, it was the only spot of colour in the room that was otherwise devoid of personality.

"It's just as bad in the living room," she informed Herb. "Let me show you."

She grabbed the little plant – which she now realised was in a white pot – and toured him through the living room. The carpet was an extension of the meditation room, and faded in its own unique window pattern, barely adding a touch of diversity to the interior.

"Taupe," she grumbled at the plant. "The couch is taupe. They shouldn't call it that. It's lying. This is just another shade of white. Dressed up, empty, soulless white. And the cushions are no better." She scowled at the cushions which had been tinted with the faintest whisper of blue. Thanks to the sun in the windows, the faint pastel was also fading to white.

She pointed Herb at the table. "We have one table. One. It's glass. And guess what colour the chairs are?"

With a huff she stalked to the bedroom.

"And here it's all grey. The most colourful, interesting decoration in the entire flat is grey. The colour of depression and dark clouds."

She could hear her voice scratching towards the inaudible, where dog whistles sounded. Her face burned. She wished she was crying. Tears would be a relief. Instead, they sucked inward, like the sucking anonymity of her flat. She could practically feel it draining her soul through the tendrils of carpet.

"The entire flat needs a change," she announced. With a clunk, she banged Herb down on the side table.

"I'm going to go down to the stores." She added. The thought gave her a brief flutter in her chest.

Amid all those tourist shops there are dozens of places that call themselves home décor, but she had never been into any of them. Her skin crawled at the thought of the suffocating layers of perfume they sprayed on every surface, and the narrow eyes of the bored shop assistants who silently judged you.

But the flat was worse. She needed new pillows, new sheets, something to hang on the wall, a lamp, anything to break the emotional sterility of her asylum-like home. She threw off her pyjamas and, without so much as a splash of water in her face, shoved on some clothes and her coat.

She glanced at Herb on her way out of the bedroom and stopped.

"And I am getting you a new pot," she decided. "Something colourful."

She grabbed her umbrella and fled outside before her will slipped again.

The narrow roads to the high streets were, thankfully, empty. It saved her the constant worry of how high to raise or lower her umbrella to allow people through. An antique shop on the corner caught her eye first, but she decided to press on to one of the smaller tourist shops. Everything in the window was wood. She needed something a bit livelier than mahogany.

A few doors down she noticed a store with toys and books clustered in the windows. They were mostly pastel, but shone in layers of green, orange, yellow and blue. She ducked in before she could overthink it. This was colour and she needed colour.

On entering, A cheerful man at the till looked up from his paper and grinned. "Come in and dry off!" he clambered, filling the space with his cheerful voice. "Nice day for shopping."

She'd made the wrong decision. Her heart sank. But she also knew she couldn't just turn around and leave.

Ursula made a noise of agreement as she closed her umbrella. The need to make conversation pressed firmly against her skull, but not a single word popped out of her brain.

The burning embarrassment of leaving so soon got the better of her. Biting hard on the inside of her cheeks, she turned to the nearest in display. A series of cheerful cards pulsating with reds and pinks stared back at her.

"Have the day off today?" The shopkeeper asked.

She could practically feel his eyes boring into her.

"Yeah," Ursula replied, hoping her short answer would send the right message. Instead, the man lingered, blinking at her with eyes that seemed to poke her in the ribs. A nervous tremor circled her stomach, and she found herself adding:

"Actually, I have two weeks off from work."

"Ah, you are here on holiday," his smile twisted wider, doubling in size. It reminded her of the large toads that engulfed entire cities in Australia.

"You picked a bad time for it, I'm afraid," The man continued. "Supposed to be wet all week. But it's a great chance to try all the restaurants." As he listed the cafes and pubs along the main road, his voice seemed to fade away as though a great distance was spreading out between him.

The way he spoke wasn't aggressive, yet she could feel each additional word fill the air between them, crushing her under his presence. The weight of his words pressed into her side. Her lungs cried out for space. Her eyes glanced to the door which was feet away and felt like an impossible distance. There was no way out.

Her mind tried to spring into action. Other people must know what to do, what to say, or how to act to escape these social shackles. But the answer didn't appear. Her mind was thrumming in her ears. Or was that her heart?

Her hips pressed into the display, pinning her in place. Suddenly, she felt dizzy.

"Do you like fish?" he asked, commanding her shredding attention. Unable to find her words, Ursula nodded.

"Ahh then you really need to go down to the cob. Get a nice bit of fried fish and walk the Cob. Not today, of course. But when the weather clears up."

"Thanks," Ursula managed to squeak. She took an uncertain step backwards and ran into a table. The shop was smaller than it seemed from outside. She swallowed hard in an effort to right herself.

"Do you happen to sell pots?" She managed to ask. "You know, for plants?"

"Oh, are you a gardener, then? You might do better at the garden centre, they have all manner of sizes." The man bobbed his way forward, nearly touching her as he squeezed by. She could see his pores.

"No," Ursula forced her voice to speak. She took a step back, letting him stride ahead. The space was warm with the heat of his body.

"I just have the one house plant," she continued, babbling. "It's kind of small."

"Ah, just starting out. Well, it starts with one, but before you know it, you'll have dozens. Everyone is getting into plants these days," he commented. He turned back to her and waved a hand over the few feet of distance.

"Come on then," he smirked. A glint in his eyes made it seem like he had just assumed something about her. She couldn't imagine what.

"Decorative pots are at the back," he pointed over his shoulder, "I don't have many but some of the small vases and ceramic pencil holders will do too."

Ursula hesitated. He was standing in her path. Her throat tightened. The air was too thin. It was only hitting the very top of her lungs.

She dove past the shopkeeper and leapt to the back wall, nearly crashing into the round display table. She barely registered the different options, grabbing the nearest pot she could see.

"That one's a mug, not a pot," The man commented. She found she couldn't reply. His words floated around her, pushed in the air closer to her face, suffocating her with heat.

Silently she dragged herself to the register to pay. He kept talking. There was something more about the mug. With a weak smile she tapped her card on the machine and shoved the pink ceramic tube into her handbag.

The door seemed too far away, but when she reached out for the handle it was there. She lurched out into the cold, fresh air with a surge of relief. The rain whipped at her face, and she was briefly thankful for the shock of cold. Her body slowly leached out the pent-up heat in her body. She felt the rain run down her hair and soak into her shirt. Once she could feel the frigid air flow down to the base of her lungs, she slowly opened her umbrella.

In a daze, she turned back the way she came, and followed the road home. She could feel her legs chill as the rain soaked through her jeans until her thighs were almost burning, but she dragged herself up the hill and back to her flat. Getting through the door she didn't feel any drier. Her energy had long gone, left behind on the pavement somewhere. She dropped her bag to the floor on the way to the bathroom.

She barely made it into the door of the small, tiled room before she peeled off her jeans and threw them into a heap on the floor. She looked down at her thighs. Each had a long oval of pink where the wet jeans had chilled her skin. Strange, she thought to herself, that she couldn't feel it.

She made her way to the bed and curled up on the soft surface, eyes unfocused on the plain grey white of her wall. Time, most likely, passed. If it did, it went around her fixed spot on the bed.

At some point she realised what she needed to do. Perhaps the thought had been there all along. It was madness not to meditate. It had saved her before. It could do so now. It was the only way to keep her emotions from crawling over her skin like a thousand tiny insects. It felt like the only way to survive.

Ursula spread herself out on the bed and let her eyes unfocus over the wide ceiling. She concentrated on the weight of her body supported by the bed and could feel the folds of her duvet caught behind her back and her legs. With each breath she sank deeper. Eventually, her shoulders rolled back and her jaw released. She could sense the individual muscles along her spine release. She drowned out the thud of her heartbeat with the sound of her breath.

Once she could only hear the draw of air in and out of her lungs, she closed her eyes. Despite the rain, the afternoon light sunk through her eyelids, tinting the darkness faintly orange. The colour seemed to ebb and flow with her breath, spreading out like ripples in a pond.

It happened so easily. The orange grew stronger, brighter, and paler. Her eyes flooded with marigold, lined with the tiny red veins on the backs of her eyes. It faded, almost to white as the expanse of sand spread across her vision with the clarity of reality. Each grain of sand was as vivid and distinct as the hairs on her arms.

The desert had become beautiful in her absence. The parched land webbed with cracks looked almost like the smooth stone tiles of a floor. The sand shone like diamonds flickering in the wind. The sky looked luminous, glowing with diffused pure sunlight.

Her chest expanded with awe as she watched the winds pick up its usual curl of sand. The delicate dance of infinitesimal grains made her chest well with warmth. The desert, she realised, was part of her. Of everything. The sand, the air, the earth, the sky, moving in a predestined symbiosis. The grains like her own blood cells jostling and moving to keep the surface alive. The wind moved with her breath. The ground reflected a subtle warmth onto her body. Everything was in sync.

When her hand appeared before her in the shimmering black of the bodysuit, she felt the same rush of connection at seeing the hundreds of scales in perfect tessellation. Her hand moved, sending the sparks of blue dancing across her. The precision of it was like watching the petals of a flower bloom in perfect time with one another. An exact symmetry of nature was hidden in the suit, in the sand, and in the desert. Harmony echoed like a gong through her body.

And then the desert collapsed, fading back to the grey of her eyelids. The heat had vanished, and she once more felt the chill of damp on her skin. Her breath was once again the only noise in her ears. As she blinked herself back into the cold grey world of her flat, she felt a soft tug at her heart. This was not the sharp pain that had ended the last two visions, but a melancholic pull of her soul. A tear formed in her closed eyes as Ursula broke out into a wide, joyous smile.

***

The next day Ursula looked forward to meditation. She found herself awake before the alarm and sprang off to her room. The sun was just rising, blushing the sky and the ocean world pink and purple. The rooftiles shimmered with blue. It reminded her of a pastel version of the suit in her vision. She wanted to go back.

The routine of following her breath was easy to get into, but when her alarm finally sounded twenty minutes later, nothing had happened. The time had passed, she had been lost in her breath, easy to let go when her thoughts flitted elsewhere; but that was all.

It's not going to happen every time, she told herself, ignoring a ball of disappointment lodged in her ribcage.

The day went by smoothly as well. Herb was re-potted. The pink of the mug matched his buds enough to give him a flush of new health and life. He seemed better for it. Ursula wrapped her meditation bolster in an old shirt, giving the taupe of her meditation room a splash of blue.

She walked along the beach and collected colourful bits of stone and a chunk of driftwood to add to her shelves. She meditated again at lunch, which she'd never done before. And again, before bed, which she had when the EHS was at its worst.

Two more days went by that way.

She went back into town and returned home with a velvet orange blanket and some mustard cushions. She had enough groceries for the week.

It crossed her mind to call Jill. But she would be pleased the visions had stopped, though, in the end, she called Rob.

"I get it. I get it," he insisted after she told him about meditating a second time. "You think you've proved the meditation is what triggers them, not the Reader."

"Haven't I?" Ursula found herself smiling.

"Not if you haven't been able to do it again," he reminded her. "In fact, the time away from the Reader might be exactly why you haven't had any more."

"I don't think so," she insisted. "I think it's emotional. All the times I have had these visions I've been upset, or anxious. I was nervous about going to work – vison; I had just been reviewing an intense nightmare – vision; and then a few days ago I was on the edge of a panic attack."

"But the third time you were relaxed, hanging out on the beach."

"Okay, not perfect, but most of the time I'm anxious or upset, what if that makes me more…" Ursula struggled to find the right phrase. It wasn't vulnerability or anger or fear, but there was something around each of these words that made the connection. She could sense she was close to the answer.

"Actually," Rob disrupted her thinking. "You may have a point. What you're saying might to match up with some things I've found.

"They let you see the Dreamer files?" Ursula asked. A rush of excitement scattered along her spine.

"Don't get too excited," he warned. "There was little I could access since I'm in IT. The files that that I could access were heavily redacted. There's no way to tell gender, age, or even how many subjects there are."

"Oh," Ursula replied. The word fell out of her mouth like a lead weight.

"But I found something that might be more important."

"What?" Ursula felt a tiny jump in her chest.

"I tried a few ways to access the Dreamer files – going through the IT side, going through the lab – and I eventually decided to try to route through you."

"What do you mean, me?"

"By going through your files and seeing what documents were attached, what files you have access to, that kind of thing."

"You said you didn't want to invade anyone's privacy."

"I basically already had your permission," he reminded her.

Although Rob couldn't see it, Ursula shrugged. He was right.

"The thing is..." he trailed off.

Ursula waited; suddenly aware of how long each second was.

"I couldn't find you," he finally admitted.

"You have a username and password; you have a pass ID; but they don't connect to personnel files, employment history, or anything else in the employee database. I couldn't even find your commissary record."

"What does that mean, I'm not technically an employee?" Ursula's stomach buzzed with a sick vibration. They were already preparing to fire her, she thought. This break was just a façade.

"No; actually, it's weirder than that. The only other elements on the system that are buried in this way are the files on the development of the Medusa machine. When we trained, they told us that the research and development files were protected by literally not being on the system. They aren't linked to any account or personnel in the way that, say, my calendar and notes are linked to my login.

"Instead, they put all the files for each Cygnet on one computer with a physical hard-drive backup. No cloud connection, no internet. It is nearly un-hackable because you need to go to that specific computer to access the information."

Rob paused as though waiting for Ursula to say something, but she couldn't come up with a word. Her brain was frozen. She could feel it struggling to take in what he had said, let alone process the information. Her tongue seemed glued to the bottom of her mouth.

"I think this means that part of the Medusa experiment is you." Rob's voice was firm. It didn't have any of the usual energy of one of his theories; instead, he seemed to be impressing each word on Ursula carefully so his meaning could not be skewed.

"*I'm* the experiment," Ursula echoed. She hoped saying it out loud would help the words sink into her mind. Still, it produced nothing.

"What if the Medusa and your Reader were not made to read dreams; what if using the Readers is supposed to alter and enhance your mind?"

"What about the dreamers?" Ursula asked numbly. "They are in the system, and they use the Medusa."

She felt like a child unable to grasp a simple concept.

"Again, as far as I can tell, there is only one Dreamer. I still have more to look into, but I wonder if you need another person's unconscious in order to have your half of the Medusa project work. What if reading dreams is an exercise for your mind, and the more you read them, the stronger certain parts of your brain or your unconscious become. I think that's why the Dreamer has files in the main database, but you don't. You are probably on the R&D computer. Test Subject 1."

"That would be illegal," Ursula's voice squeaked. "Swan would have to tell me if they were experimenting on me."

"They *should*," Rob agreed, "but it doesn't always work that way. If it helps the experiment for you to be unaware of what is going on, then they would make sure you didn't know anything. It happens in psychological experiments. Like the Milgram experiment."

"I don't live in the conspirosphere, Rob. What is the Milgram experiment?"

"It's not a conspiracy, it was an actual psychological experiment at Yale University in, I think, the 1960s. They brought people to a room with a button in it – or some machine – and told them that if they hit the button, it would give an unseen person in the next room an electric shock. A person dressed like a doctor then told them to press the button over and over again, increasing the electric dose in between each time. To the people in the experiment, it seemed like the pain was becoming more and more extreme – sometimes life threatening. And yet, they would keep pushing the button when told to.

"In reality, though, there was no second person being electrocuted. It was all a lie. The psychologists were testing everyone in the room with the button. They wanted to know if people would be more likely to hurt someone if someone in authority gave them permission. So, you see, a little misinformation was essential."

"That was the 1960s. And in a psychology lab. This is a company in the 21st century. It would be illegal to lie to me about my job. It's not worth the risk."

"Maybe it is to them," Rob replied gravely. She knew there was no point arguing; Rob had never trusted any company, why try to convince him now?

"Okay, but more to the point, there is no reason to think I am the experiment. I go into the lab to get equipment updates; I submit all the dream information; it's basically any other beta testing job, aside from the equipment."

"Except that you are having visions."

Ursula paused. She was having visions; that was the point of their call, and why Rob had dug into the files. She was certain they were visions; not dreams or panic attacks, whatever Jill might say. The lack of pain now seemed to support that idea, and her last visit to the desert felt like a message. It felt real, and peaceful. For a moment it felt like being welcomed home.

"What if your vision of the desert was what they expected to happen?" Rob continued after a moment. "Maybe something similar happened before but your mind was so upset by it that it started these panic attacks? It might be why your memory is screwed up. Playing with someone's mind is unheard of, so it is going to be risky. They stopped things, and once the panic receded, you started seeing the visions properly."

"This isn't making any sense." Ursula's brain might as well have been filled with molasses; everything she heard was getting stuck.

"Okay let's take this step by step. You had these dessert visions when you were meditating, or after being on the Reader, right?"

"Yes." There was a sense of relief at having a question that was easy to answer.

"And you always meditate before you use the Reader?"

"It's more like a mindfulness exercise. I focus on my breath and on my body, so I don't lose myself in the dream."

"But basically, the mental state before you have visions is the same," Rob summarised.

"I said that a minute ago: it's not just meditating, I'm upset just before it happens."

"Except the beach – not to harp on about it; but I think that's relevant. It seems to me that you are emotionally open. Sometimes that's because you are upset or anxious, but sometimes it's like that moment on the beach; deeply relaxed. In all cases you seem emotionally open."

"And what does that have to do with my files being hidden on the Swan computers?" Ursula asked. A dull throbbing was growing behind her eyes.

"Did you know that people who meditate can sometimes have visions?"

"No."

"I've read about this before," Rob explained with excitement. "It happens to gurus and monks, and a handful of people all over the world who just practice meditation regularly."

"I think that's just a myth, like levitating yogis," Ursula felt a twinge of frustration. Where was he trying to go with all this nonsense – experiments and yogis and ridiculous stories.

"It's not a myth. It's a documented phenomenon. They have recorded examples of it all over the world and for centuries. If you were meditating, or in a similar mental state, it wouldn't be impossible that you are experiencing the same thing."

"I doubt I've had a spiritual experience," Ursula grumbled. "Besides, I'm not exactly the Buddha."

"Of course not. You are too grumpy," Rob teased.

Ursula huffed impatiently.

"My point is," Rob pressed on, "that maybe your time on the Reader has been exercising the brain in the same way. You get, from a few months on a machine, the benefit of a lifetime of strict meditation and yoga: spiritual transcendence."

"The desert isn't like a visualisation exercise," Ursula sighed. "I could see every piece of sand and feel some of the heat on my body. It felt almost real."

"Visions can be very real experiences for the people who have them. There are records throughout history of visions and religious experiences that feel deeply real to the person. Hell, St Theresa famously saw God and had a religious orgasm."

"That is not helping your case."

"Urg," Rob grunted. "Right. Let's remove religion. They did a study at somewhere like the University of London where they put people meditating in an MRI machine. When the subjects had a vision, the MRI showed corresponding brain activity. So, everything they saw with their eyes closed was processed by their brain as though they were really seeing it, right in front of them."

"Really?" Ursula tossed the idea around in her mind. She had been told that meditation could increase and decrease certain areas of brain mass. She already knew it could help develop and strengthen synapses in the brain. A vision was only a step – or maybe a leap – away from either of those.

"That's hard, medical evidence," Rob concluded triumphantly. "They are doing more studies on this all the time. Some places are working on the theory – and this is important for you – that we can train the brain to induce these meditative visions."

Ursula took a deep breath.

"So, you think the Reader has restructured my brain, and that's why I am having visions?" Ursula spoke each word carefully to be sure she was summarising his theory exactly.

"I think it's possible."

"Then why am I seeing the same thing every time? I don't think that's normal for gurus? They see God or paradise. I'm seeing a dry desert, a swirl of sand in the wind, and my hands in black gloves."

"Not every vision is profound," Rob insisted. She could practically hear his patience growing thin. "And there is no reason you wouldn't see the exact same thing every time. You might be unconsciously returning to it because you want to. You called me because you miss seeing it."

Ursula wanted to argue. The first few times she was afraid of seeing the desert again. But perhaps her mind knew better. The last vision had given her a feeling of being connected. The only one she could remember. This theory might explain why she lost nearly a year to panic attacks, and why her memory was fractured and fragmented. If the Reader had been playing with her mind, it would feel jumbled.

It would also explain why Jill had been so insistent about taking her off the Reader. Most of their call had been Ursula arguing that there wasn't any association between the visions of the desert and her Reader machine; but Jill seemed to have made her mind up long before the call.

"And remember, your files are completely hidden from IT security. No one else's records are – even Mackenzie Swaiteck." Rob drove the point home.

For a moment Ursula struggled to respond. Her head seemed to float away from her body, leaving thoughts suspended somewhere in between. She leaned her back against the wall and slid to the floor.

Taking the weight off her body helped. So did closing her eyes. She tried to add Rob's point about her files to everything that had already turned her life upside down. Briefly, she was reminded of Jill's favourite mantra that the simplest solution was best. Too many strange things had been happening. This was the only option that seemed to corral all the facts.

"Say you're right," Ursula's voice broke. "What am I supposed to do now?"

"I don't know," Rob admitted. His voice was low enough to rumble through the phone. She wondered if he was curled on the floor too.

"It's up to you. You can go to them, demand the truth and to give you the help you need. You can accept that you have lost part of your memory, but stick it out on the Reader because you might be gaining new skills beyond most of us. Either way, it might be smart to get more evidence. Something to protect yourself. I'll look around."

"I wish I could get back to the desert," Ursula whispered. "I feel like the gloves are just the tip of the iceberg. If I could get back – if I could see more – I'd have a better idea of what is going on. And what to do."

"I might be able to help with that." Rob offered.

"Oh?" Ursula wasn't certain if he was teasing or serious.

"It's something that seems to have reliable results; and if you do get there, I can almost guarantee it'll last longer. But it would require doing something illegal."

"How illegal?" Ursula rolled her eyes.

***

In the end, Rob gave her mints with a micro-dose of THC, which, he explained, gave her more control as well as easing her into the experience. From what he had told her, it was a far more reliable option than mushrooms.

As they spoke Ursula found herself wondering how many psychedelics and hallucinogens Rob had tried. From their brief debate, it sounded like he had a thorough – and occasionally unpleasant – knowledge of all the options. In warning her about one he gleefully described a trip where he was convinced his teeth melted and he had to scoop them up with a spoon to bring them to the dentist. The thought made her shiver so violently, Rob heard it over the phone.

It wasn't until the weekend that he was able to come by and drop the doses off. She took him to lunch at the café as a thanks, but also to help fill the days. They were starting to drag again. At the train station he didn't seem prepared to leave. It made her wonder about the tiny mints in her purse. He would never give her something dangerous, but he was evidently a little worried.

He suggested she start with one, but she chopped the mint in half before trying it. Just in case. Still, swallowing it gave her a small thrill. It was the first illegal thing she could remember doing. Other than asking Rob to hack private files. But that had been from a distance. This was a real action she performed. It was also quite nice that know that she could do something illegal and exciting without leaving the flat.

A half hour passed, and she still didn't feel anything, so took the other half. This time it didn't feel as exciting. She felt caught in a state of boredom; unable to do anything in case it started to kick in.

With a vague hope of improving her chances of a vision, Ursula made her way to the meditation room. She gave Herb a gentle pat and settled in, looking out at the crisp blue ocean through her window. The light was high enough to be bounding off the houses and street below, making the entire village seem like summertime. The ocean was bright blue as though it were drawn in crayon. It seemed like a good sign.

She was hoping for a feeling of every muscle releasing or a deep well of calm appearing in her core. Nothing came until her left foot fell asleep. She batted at its numb flesh, wrinkling her face with each rush of tingling. She had been sitting there long enough that she could no longer flex her toes.

Once her toes were back under the control of her nervous system and the worst of the pins and needles subsided, she limped back to the living room and took two more mints.

"What could Rob have possibly been worried about?" she asked the room.

She flopped onto the sofa and made herself comfortable under the new blanket. It was soft and heated in patches by resting in the sunlight. She wondered if that was what it felt like to have fur. Wrapped in a constant soft cosiness. It was pleasant.

Her eyes rested on the ceiling. Why wasn't her ceiling smooth, she wondered. Ceilings in movies and TV shows were all smooth. If you saw them at all, it was a long stretch of white (always white). But hers had little rough dimples all over it. Like a ceiling with acne.

The thought made her giggle. A flat with acne. Had she had acne as a kid? She couldn't remember. She didn't really remember being a child. There were moments. Flashes of being hugged. Of running around. She didn't really remember other children. But she remembered loneliness. That had stuck around.

She tried to picture the house she grew up in. It probably had a flat ceiling, she thought. She remembered it being warm. A warm house in Britain. That seemed novel. The idea made her giggle again. Whether it was the thought or the blanket or the shift in the sun, her body spread with warmth. She closed her eyes and let it kiss her face. Cosy, soft, luscious, heat.

The desert faded into her eyelids seamlessly. She could tell the mints were working because every detail was intensified. She could feel the strange flush of hot and cold on her skin through the tightness of the bodysuit. It wrapped around her legs holding her in. She could breathe in the scent of the desert air mixed with something faintly metallic. It smelled of heat.

She looked for the curl of wind just before it pulled the sand from the desert floor. It was as if she had caused it to happen by simply remembering. She could see now that the whirl it created collapsed in on itself, leaving the impression of a shape it never truly formed.

To her delight, she could feel her muscles and ligaments move in sync as her right hand lifted, appearing before her face. The bodysuit, she realised, reflected not only the light, but the heat as well, cooling in puddles around her knuckles where the suit flashed blue.

She could feel the material more clearly now as well. It had the stickiness of a wetsuit, clinging to each fold in her hand and tugging at the fingernails. And yet, the internal layer of material was also coarse, scratching along her unseen arms.

As she looked on her hand beneath the black scales, she knew it was one with a larger bodysuit. She sensed the invisible seams at the wrist where the gloves met the arms and knew a similar attachment existed somewhere at her ankles. She suddenly became aware of the pressure on her toes, clutched together in the slippery socks of the suit. She could tell from the feel that they wrapped around each toe, tickling the fold between her pinkie toe and its neighbour. She wanted to smile or laugh at the sensation, but her face didn't move.

With a breath she flexed her fingers and the iridescent scales shimmered in shades of blue beneath the sun. She smiled at the familiarity of it. The elongated seconds allowed her to watch each individual scale twinkle in the sunlight, along with the rush of coolness it offered to her skin. Without actively thinking about it she became aware that each scale reflected the heat away from her skin, keeping her body cosseted in a mild and humid warmth, protected from the surrounding astringent air. It was protecting her, and she was grateful. Yet her chest didn't swell with peace. It was caught in a cold grip. Her throat thickened at the same time, and her cheeks went hot.

She was distantly aware that the vision was lasting longer. The sensations were not her own, but another piece of the strange pageant playing around her.

Ursula took a sharp breath as she watched the thumb and forefinger of her right-hand curl into an O. It took her a moment to realise she was gesturing 'OK'. Her eyes shifted focus, peering beyond the circle of her fingers and towards three looming black columns.

Her heart pounded in her ears. For a moment she wondered if they could be rocks but, as she continued to stare, the distant shadows settled into three human silhouettes. The central pillar nodded. A spray of blue cascaded over his form and spread out from the epicentre of its neck.

Her eyes flew open without any pain. She could hear the thrum of her heart in her ears, and the quick pace of her breathing.

The shadow was a person. The thought sang in her mind, blocking out any concern for calming her breath. And, she realised, they were wearing the same iridescent bodysuit.

Her first thought was that this changed everything. But did it? She wasn't sure. She reached for the phone to dial Rob, but couldn't. She didn't need his voice in her head. She needed to get a grip on what she saw. And what she thought it meant. After all it was her vision.

It was.

It had to be.

After a relentless run on the beach, she felt less certain. The main crack in her belief was the other people in her vision. Was it possible to imagine people she didn't recognise? Any strangers in her own dreams always came with a certain level of familiarity, but they were a complete unknown. The uncertainty filled her head, rejecting any other thought and keeping the exhaustion of her body from coming near her mind.

In the middle of the night, she decided she had to try again. There were only two mints left. It would have to do. She grabbed them and threw a coat over her pyjamas. The beach had helped before and she knew it would help now.

At that hour the beach was empty, and the waves were barely lapping under the cold white light of the moon. She settled in the sand, feeling a cold damp sink through the material of her trousers and into her legs.

Ursula closed her eyes and let her mind fill with the sound of the waves, crashing through her brain and taking away any lingering doubts and worries that had built up overnight. The ocean whispered, cradling her mind as the sand cradled her body. The feel of the sand morphed from the beach to the desert so smoothly it was almost imperceptible.

She welcomed the desert with an instant sense of peace. The beginning was now a well-choreographed dance; simple, precise, and controlled. Each moment was given it's beat and no longer: her eyes over the landscape, then the feel of the wind, the whorl of sand in the distance. They were like heartbeats, ending with the lift of her hand and her finger running along the seam of the suit as it burst forward in infinitesimal blue fireworks.

The gesture in the distance came with a tug – a yanking beneath her ribs either of fear or uncertainty. Her jaw tightened as the shadows settled into the clear shapes of the people in the distance. Her growing fear was suddenly jostled by a sharp tug just below her shoulder blades.

Something was behind her, pulling on a heavy weight held on her back. For the first time, she felt the weight of the straps as they pulled at her shoulders. Her breath caught – either in the vision, or reality. She willed herself to shake the pack free from her back, but the vision body remained calm and immobile. The idea passed over her that the vision-Ursula was happy to have it on. She could sense the distant calm of reassurance settle into the chest of her vision-self.

With the sound of shifting sand, a body circled around her and came into view. She could see from the contours of the tightly packed suit it was a woman, the same height as she was. As though possessed, sadness poured over her body. Her eyes sought out those of the mystery companion, but it didn't have a face. The scales of the suit stretched over the hairline and around the chin, hiding any hair and streamlining the skull into the shape of a teardrop. At the centre, where the features should be, was a detailed array of tubes twisting in a distorted, unnatural labyrinth. It was monstrous, she thought, as she realised she must look the same.

The thought made her dizzy.

The woman took her hands, turning them carefully over in her own. The stranger ran her fingers over the same seams Ursula had just been checking. Before Ursula could respond to the touch, the woman looked up. Amid the web of wires and mesh, the black goggles were a perfect mirror of black. For a moment Ursula could see her own monstrous electric face floating in them.

As prickles of nausea coursed down her skill, Ursula's earbud crackled with a female voice: "Are you ready?"

Ursula felt the neck of her body bend as her vision-self nodded. Her throat thickened and her eyes stung. It was too dry to waste hydration with crying. The figure squeezed her arm gently. Sadness hit Ursula in the chest like a cannon. She was amazed her body remained vertical.

Silently, the woman walked away, leaving Ursula disoriented and alone. She wanted to call out, to cry for the stranger to stay. Or maybe grab her and hold her against her chest so she couldn't leave.

Another voice – deeper and steadier – hissed into the suit: "Mission Daedalus commencing final checks."

Ursula's head swayed in a distorted seasickness. Her brain swelled, struggling against the inside of her skull. Her ears began to ring.

"Recording Team ready," a voice floated into the suit, just audible over the throbbing of her ears.

"Safety team ready," the female voice replied.

The words melted and bubbled in her mind oozing into nonsense.

Safe from what? She silently howled.

"Subject ready?" the man's voice booms in her ear.

"Ready." With a crush to her chest, Ursula recognised the sound of her own voice. She hadn't felt her lips move.

"Commencing in ten. Nine," the male voice continued in a sombre drone.

Her mind screamed out for home. She needed to get back. To the ocean, to the town, and to the safety of her flat. Grappling with the edges of her body, Ursula urged her soul to return, searching for the feel of sand beneath her toes; she was straining to hear any distance hum of the ocean.

"Eight. Seven. Six."

They warned her. Her mind offers this thought up like a last gasp of air. Jill had warned her, this was dangerous. She shouldn't have come back to the desert.

"Five. Four."

A scream of frustration blistered in her throat, but her mouth wouldn't open.

"Three."

I need to wake up, her mind screamed. *I have to get out of here*. But her arms wouldn't thrash and her legs didn't run. She was trapped.

"Two."

All the resistance released at once. Like a bracing rush of water, the thought coated her body: *this is going to kill me.*

"One."

Fire engulfed her brain. Her body stretched from both sides, pulled like a rubber band old enough to crack under the pressure. An explosion of agony shredded every cell. Her body smeared across the desert, wringing her breath from her body as her vision skittered. Colours melted into one another, pouring into a teary fog of blackness. She was agony. She was death. Her heart stopped. Her lungs failed. Her mind wailed into oblivion.

It was over before she could scream. With a blink, the ocean was still there, calmly rustling against the sand. Her body pitched forward reflexively, shoving her face into the sand. She smelled the sea and sand mix as she added the acrid smell of her own vomit.

Jill

With a shaking hand, Jill put down her phone and closed her eyes. She had managed to calm Ursula down enough to wait for a session tomorrow. It had felt like a punch to the gut delaying the session, but she needed time to think.

A creak of the door let her know that Mackenzie had come into the kitchen. She opened her eyes and looked across the expanse of pink marble and greying wood to her partner. She seemed calm, but her mouth was stretched into a grim, flat line.

"That was Ursula," Mackenzie remarked. Her tone suggested she had tried and failed to make it sound like a question.

Jill realised her partner had been eavesdropping but couldn't muster the will to be upset about it. The anguish and terror in Ursula's strained voice was still too vivid in her mind.

"She had another vision," Jill confirmed. "The pain was worse this time."

It was an effort to keep her voice steady. She looked down at her hands and found her left one itching at her wrist. Had that happened since Mackenzie came in?

"Was it as extreme as when she had the panic attacks?" Her partner asked. She was still hovering by the door uncertainly.

"It sounded brutal," Jill choked on the words.

"Is she okay?" Mackenzie asked. Her voice was unnaturally calm. It grated.

"For now. I'll know more when I see her tomorrow," Jill replied and went in search of a bottle of wine. She needed something to temper the emotions wrestling inside her. She could feel them jostle in her chest, rearranging her organs.

"It's only been a few days; it could still be the effects of the Reader," Mackenzie stated.

Jill sighed.

"Can we not talk about this right now," she asked Mackenzie, her eyes still on the rack of bottles. There were only three, but she couldn't decide.

"I can give you a few minutes, but we need to talk about it before you see her again."

Jill closed her eyes and shook her head. Mackenzie was right, but Jill didn't want her to be. She grabbed a bottle blindly and brought it to the table. The few steps winded her. She slumped into one of the beechwood recycled chairs and her shoulders slumped. The only thing she felt capable of was staring at the table, where the lines in the wood danced around a round knot.

She listened as Mackenzie got out two glasses and placed them on the table. With a muted squeak the cork pulled loose. Mackenzie filled both glasses, higher than usual. Silently she passed one along to Jill. She took a long sip.

"I don't know what is happening to Ursula anymore," Jill admitted. She stared into the reflective surface of the wine, watching her face bend over the curved ruby surface.

Mackenzie drew a breath and held it, not speaking.

"Deep down I knew this break wasn't going to be a permanent solution," Jill continued, her voice shaking in a blend of sadness and anger. "The hypnosis has failed. And I've sent her away to deal with it on her own."

"That's not fair," Mackenzie objected.

"That's right, I didn't do it; we did. You practically made me do it." Her words were trembling now, but she no longer cared.

"It's only been a week. This could still be an effect of the machine, in which case sending her away was the right move." Mackenzie insisted, ignoring the jab.

"She's remembering more," Jill glared at Mackenzie. "She told me that the vision is getting longer. She saw shadows in the desert this time. What if she sees who they are?"

"She hasn't yet," Mackenzie reminded her. "And things may still improve."

Jill snorted, careful to keep her eyes steady on her partner, demanding better answers with the force of her look.

"And if the hypnosis is failing," Mackenzie continued, "time away from the Medusa project, from us, and anything else that might trigger her memory is a promising idea. If only to slow down the process."

"That's the best we are hoping for? To slow down what's happening to her?" Jill's voice was sharp as steel.

"It's a start," Mackenzie took a drink, breaking away from Jill's gaze.

"This is serious, Kenzie. We cannot keep pretending everything is fine." Jill found her voice growing louder.

"I am aware of how serious this is, Jill," Mackenzie replied coldly.

"Then stop saying it is going to be okay. It isn't okay."

"We don't know exactly what happened. Until you see her tomorrow, I am trying to keep an objective perspective."

"You are trying to stay in control," Jill knew the words would sting. She wanted them to.

"You're right," Mackenzie kept her voice restrained but put her wineglass down with enough force to make the glass waver. "I am trying to control the situation. Because you know what happens if I don't?"

"You can't control it –"

"If I don't, we lose everything." Mackenzie's voice boomed over Jill's. The force of it shocked her backwards. "She could be found. The company would be over. We could all be arrested. And Ursula will be taken. You can imagine what they would do to her. Not to mention we could all be killed."

The room seemed to echo with Mackenzie's words.

"I am trying to protect you. And I am trying to protect her," she concluded.

Jill swallowed her tears.

"I'm sorry. I know," Jill's voice was weak. "It just feels like we are wrong, and we are waiting too long to see it. I think we are already in danger."

The pink left Mackenzie's face, but she didn't speak.

"I thought time away would at least help with the pain," Jill whined. The tracks of her tears burnt in rows over cheeks. "Instead, everything is still getting worse, and we don't know what to do."

The question crackled in the air. She knew there wasn't an answer. They knew no more now than they did when Ursula first had a flash of the desert. It felt like years ago.

"We need to move your office," Mackenzie suddenly realised.

"I can't," Jill replied. "You know that I can't."

"I think that's exactly why you should," Mackenzie replied.

Jill could see the energy course through Mackenzie's limbs, reflecting a growing enthusiasm for the idea. It was a sign that Mackenzie was becoming certain.

"I promised," Jill put as much weight into the two words as she could muster. It was shocking that Mackenzie would consider such an idea.

"I know, but the situation has changed," Mackenzie insisted. "Like you said, the hypnosis is failing. What we need now is to mitigate the damage. We can strike a balance with things and once she is stable you can redo the hypnosis. Fully. Not a little repair job, the entire thing."

"Why do you think anything will get better if I move out of my office?"

"If she is remembering, don't you think being in that room might be making it worse?" Mackenzie pressed.

"She has been coming to that room for nearly a year without any sign of remembering." Jill countered.

"So, the room didn't start her memories returning; but now that she is remembering, it isn't going to help. She is going to be looking at that closet tomorrow, and at every session you have from now on."

"Ursula has never once glanced at that closet." Jill shook her head, but inside she wondered. She would never admit it to Mackenzie, but Ursula seemed to be looking too closely at her walls at the last session. She had claimed to be stretching, but Jill had never seen her do it before.

"You are in denial," Mackenzie pleaded. For the first time Jill could hear the pain in her voice.

"It's not denial if you have proof. The proof is that Ursula doesn't know." Jill doubled down; it wasn't worth speculating now.

"But she might suspect soon." Mackenzie reached out to Jill as though she was offering a rope out of the dungeon. Jill could see how certain Mackenzie was that this was the answer. It was just as clear to Jill that she was wrong.

"I understand what you are saying," Jill turned on her therapeutic voice. "You feel we need to do something, and I agree with that in principle. We need to protect her and ourselves. But I don't think this is the right thing to do."

"How can you say that? It makes sense. We take her out of anything that could strike a memory. Let her settle and then you can come in and repair the damage."

"Moving my offices would be a violation of her trust."

"No," Mackenzie's eyes narrowed. "It would be helping her."

"Before we did all of this, Ursula only asked me one thing. That closet is my responsibility." Jill put her hand against her chest to emphasise the point.

"I promised her. And if I let anyone else use this room, I would be breaking her trust."

"You would still be looking after it; just from a distance," Mackenzie replied limply. Jill knew she had won.

"And might I point out that bringing someone else into my office is also asking for trouble. They just need to drop a pen in the right place, and we could lose everything." Jill took another sip of wine. There was no way for her partner to argue. It was her only victory in weeks. No matter how trivial, she deserved to recognise it.

"We all discussed this before," Jill crowed. "Ursula and I agreed that this was the safest option."

"Ursula and you." Mackenzie threw up her arms.

"Not this again." Jill slammed down her wine, cracked the stem of the glass. The shaft split evenly in two. It was almost too perfect a metaphor.

"Yes, *this*. It's the elephant in the room," Mackenzie seethed. "This entire conversation you have talked about nothing but Ursula. What she wanted, what you promised her. But she didn't burst into your life, she burst into mine."

Jill tried to interrupt but Mackenzie threw her hand out to stop her.

"I brought you into all of this, it's my fault, you're right. But at the start, it brought us closer. We were a team. We built Swan together; it's the combination of our surnames."

"That was Ursula's idea," Jill remarked pointedly.

Mackenzie gasped as though Jill had struck her.

"She wasn't supposed to still be around, Jill. None of this was supposed to happen. We should be taking care of our own children, not babysitting a grown woman. We shouldn't be fighting about how to manage her and risking our lives, our work, and our marriage."

"We are all she has," Jill burst out.

Anger pulsed in her veins, seeping through her pores. How dare Mackenzie?

"What did you want to do?" Jill demanded. "Turn her away? *Thanks for the information, now you're on your own in a dangerous world where the government will probably torture you. But that's not my problem.* She changed everything and we owe her anything we have now."

"Then why is it always the two of you, not all three of us?" Mackenzie spat back.

"You know why."

She had been over this too many times before. When Ursula started to have the panic attacks, Jill was the only person she could turn to. She had the training and the skills to help. Back then Mackenzie was willing to do anything to help. Now she wasn't listening.

Jill looked into Mackenzie's eyes trying to plead what she could not say, but saw the anger sketched on every line of her partner's face. The muscles were so tense and twisted that her jaw could have split from her skin. It was a look Jill had never seen before.

"Fine," Mackenzie stood up. "You know her best. I'm sure you'll figure out what to do."

She was out of the room before Jill could reply. She listened in silence as Mackenzie stalked out the front door. There was no point in going after her, Jill decided, she had to prepare for her next session with Ursula. She still had no idea what to do.

Ursula

Ursula arrived at the Cygnet 7 building exhausted. She had wrestled all night with images of the three silhouettes counting down her death. She relived that final moment before her body split and warped knowing that they were causing it. With each reiteration her mind devised a new reason why they were putting her through the strange ritual. It was a punishment, torture, a strange medical procedure, a ceremonial rite, a twisted experiment. Each time, the pain was made worse with the sombre knowledge that she was a willing participant.

When the sun rose and she dragged herself from bed, echoes of the vision followed her. The pale morning sunrise reminded her of the desert light. The flakes that fell from her toast reminded her of the whirlwind of sand in the breeze. The weather also seemed against her. The spring sunlight was low and brilliant, blinding her eyelids white and burning into her skin.

The thoughts swirled inside her, causing her skin to prickle despite the mild weather. Judging from the looks she got on the near-empty train, she looked as harassed as she felt. It wasn't even a relief to arrive at the Cygnet 7 building. Instead, she found her heart thrumming erratically and her blood bouncing through her body with a ferocious cat-like energy.

To release the cacophony of energy, she bypassed the elevator and jogged up the six flights of stairs to the therapy floor. The excursion of it forced her heart into a regular rhythm, but that was the only difference. As she opened the door from the stairwell, her mind was buzzing so frenetically that she nearly ran into someone. They had not quite collided, but their bodies came close enough to feel the brush of cotton from the stranger's clothing on her hands.

Ursula jumped back, an act so sharp it startled the woman in front of her. The stranger raised a manicured hand to the chest of her burgundy suit as her mouth dropped into a small oval. Something in the eyes – wide though they were – registered with Ursula. The face as well – perhaps something about the nose or the wispy red hair pulled back into a low ponytail. Her mind sparked and bristled, but for all its energy she could not produce the woman's name. Unsure what to do or say, Ursula settled on a shaky smile.

"Excuse me," the woman offered, politely. "I didn't realise many people took the stairs."

Neither of them moved. Though her words were kind, the stranger's eyes narrowed. Two thoughts popped into Ursula's churning mind: this woman didn't recognise her, and she was expecting Ursula to say or do something. That was why she hadn't moved out of the way. Embarrassment climbed to the top of Ursula's emotional pile.

"I have an appointment," Ursula stammered. An uncomfortable heat spread over her back and up to her cheeks.

"Of course," the woman nodded briskly. As though it was the password, the stranger stood aside and held open the door for Ursula to pass through.

Eyes on the floor, Ursula ducked into the hall. As she heard the door close, she realised she had just been face-to-face with the founder of Swan. She paused. Why would Mackenzie Swaiteck be here? She couldn't imagine the head of the company using the same therapists as her employees. She probably wasn't required to do a mental health check-in, but if she did, why would she come to Cygnet 7? She worked in the main headquarters on the other side of the city.

Ursula's head started to throb just above her eyebrow. She pressed her fingers into the spot and tried to massage away the pain. She had enough to worry about without poking her nose into someone else's business – especially, the woman who ran the company. With a deep breath in she made her way to the familiar door, but when she turned the handle, it didn't move. She looked up at the small light bulb that was installed where a peephole might be. It was off. If Jill was in session, or busy, it would be glowing red. Again, Ursula jostled the handle, but it didn't budge.

Reflexively, she checked her watch. She was only a couple minutes early; Jill must have already been in the building. For a moment she listened for the sound of any further steps on the stairs, but the hall was quiet. Maybe she was taking the elevator, Ursula decided. She took a step back to move to the elevator when she noticed the nameplate on the door read "Dr Nilan".

Suddenly off balance, she looked at the door behind her only to find another name she didn't recognise. Thinking of Mrs Swaiteck, she wondered if she had she got off on the wrong floor. Her eyes went immediately to the therapy light. She was definitely on the mental health floor. But where had Jill's door gone? She felt sure her therapist would have told her if she'd moved offices.

She looked down the long hallway. It seemed to bow before her eyes, but she could tell the floor was empty. She could see all the way along the grey carpet to the silver elevator doors. Seeing them, the hallway snapped back into place. The creepy anxiety flushed away. She smiled at her mistake.

Coming up the stairs had taken her to the floor through the back entrance. She just needed to reverse her usual route. Re-orienting herself, Ursula walked along the left side of the hallway until she found the sign for Dr Annan, four doors along. As she reached for the handle, her conversation with Rob popped in her head, but before she could figure out why, the door opened.

"I thought I heard you. Come in," Jill greeted her.

Ursula took a few steps into the room. Seeing it, smelling the familiar scent of cotton that always seemed present, her stomach unclenched slightly. As she sat on the sofa, the buzzing in her ears seemed to soften as well.

"How are you doing, Ursula?" Jill asked, settling in opposite her. Ursula noticed briefly that there was no camera in its usual spot over Jill's shoulder. That, too, was a relief.

"I feel – I don't know – shaken," Ursula replied. The word came to mind because her hands were softly vibrating, but it was apt; she felt like soda that had been shaken until it was about to explode.

"Oh of course you are," Jill's eyes frowned in sympathy. "It sounded awful over the phone. But I want to say you did the best thing in calling me. You shouldn't have to go through this alone."

Ursula was uncertain what to say. Nothing Jill said had been wrong, but it also made her feel like a child in the most unpleasant way.

"If you feel up to it, I'd like to go over again."

"Oh, yes," Ursula found herself uncertain how to begin. Between the new pieces of the vision and the pain, it seemed impossible to express everything. Before she knew it tears were swelling in her eyes.

"It's okay, Ursula," Jill offered her a box of tissues. "Don't worry, you are safe here. I want you to take a few deep breaths with me now, okay?"

Jill led Ursula in a familiar breathing exercise. After Ursula counted the length of the last breath her stomach was squirming, but her hands no longer trembled.

"The most important thing for you to know right now, is that you are safe," Jill reassured her. "You are completely safe here, and we are going to everything we can to help you."

"Of course," Ursula answered. Despite everything else cluttering her mind, she noted that Jill kept saying 'we'. Her therapist had never used the plural that way before.

"I also want to apologise for not realising how serious this was the first time you came to me," Jill continued, her voice barely wavered before she regained control.

"How serious is this?" Ursula asked nervously. It was disorienting to see Jill fighting so hard to stay composed.

"Don't worry, you are going to be just fine," Jill assured her.

"But I will admit that we didn't expect these visions to keep happening once you took some time away. I am here to do everything I can for you, and we are going to find a solution for this."

Again, the word 'we' hit Ursula's ear wrong.

"Let's start slowly though." Jill paused to take out a notebook she had wedged between herself and the arm of a chair. Ursula's throat tightened. Jill hadn't used a notebook before.

"I want to understand as best I can what happened with this new vision. What were you doing when it came on?"

"I was lying on the sofa," Ursula replied carefully. She knew before she arrived that she would be too embarrassed to admit the truth about the mints. Besides, she didn't want to get Rob in trouble. Still, the small lie caused her stomach to flutter.

"Okay," Jill coaxed her, "and did the vision happen suddenly?"

"It was more gradual," Ursula commented, but didn't continue. Her stomach was twisting. She wanted to be telling Jill about what happened, but at the same time things kept popping into her mind that made her nervous. Why had she been saying 'we'? Why was she using a notebook? The sense of safety that had welcomed her into the room seemed to chip away with each question.

Yet, a voice, slowly growing in the back of her mind, warned her that this was the road back to anxiety, to paranoia. Questions were drowning her and making the world spin. In the end, they meant nothing; they were mental yokes to weight her down and keep her from feeling safe.

"Why don't you tell me what happened next?" Jill encouraged. Her eyes looked wet, but sincere.

She had always trusted Jill. She had trusted her when things were dire, and it had saved her life.

The words came out slowly and halted, her mind racing ahead of her lips. She stood up and paced to try and expel some of her overflowing nerves. As she got to the moment where she saw the figures in the distance, tears were streaming down her face. She reached for the tissues on the edge of Jill's desk. As she dabbed at her eyes, she saw a flicker of light.

She looked up. Just beyond the desk, where the wall met the carpet, there was a glint of light. She leaned over slightly and watched the reflective surface stretch into a silver line, making a smooth lip of about a meter long in the middle of the wall.

It was Rob's door.

"Ursula are you alright?" Jill was looking suspiciously at Ursula.

How long, Ursula wondered, had she been silent? She balled the tissue on her fist and turned to face Jill, careful not to glance back at the spot where the lip was.

"Yes. Sorry. I was trying to remember something whilst wiping my eyes." Ursula looked out the window as she tried to compose her face. She counted to three, hoping that was longer than she had been staring at the metal lip in the floor.

"Sorry I had it in my mind a moment ago," Ursula murmured. She let out an exhausted sigh and turned back to the sofa and walked slowly to the couch, careful not to glance back at the wall.

She sat and put her head in her hands. Jill's patient breathing seemed to echo throughout the room. In the tense silence Ursula tried to reason with herself. Sage had said the door was most likely storing patient files. Jill was the head of the department, so it made sense she might have everything in a large closet. But, as she and Rob had pointed out at the time, there was no reason to have storage that large.

She tried to force herself to find another explanation. One that had nothing to do with her visions and her broken memory, and the fact that there were no files on her in the entirety of the Swan database. Remembering the files, she felt ill. That's where they must be, all her files, her notes, and any proof they were experimenting on her must be hidden on an onsite computer – that's what Rob said. Of course, it would be in her therapist's room. Her hands felt like ice against her face.

That's why I saw Mrs Swaiteck here, she thought suddenly. *She must be part of this.*

Everything clicked with a revolting clarity. That is why Jill kept saying 'we'. They had just been talking about her. They needed a plan because they expected the visions, but not the pain. Or maybe they had expected the pain. Or maybe there was more to all of this. Her mind couldn't decide on the exact reason and explanation, but she knew it was all connected.

Her body drained of all emotion and feeling. She looked up at Jill, whose every feature reflected concern. It seemed so genuine, and yet that no longer touched her. Her soul had retracted like a turtle, hiding in the depths of her body. Everything that happened on the outside bounced off the shell of her body.

"Would you like some water?" Jill finally broke the silence. Ursula realised she had spent too long in her own mind.

"No," Ursula replied. To her ears the words sounded distant and distorted, like the sounds you hear when submerged in water.

"Sorry, I think I lost the train of thought."

"You had just seen a gloved hand make the OK sign," Jill offered, mimicking the gesture.

"Right," Ursula blinked. Her body felt like it was floating. Jill seemed to get further and further away.

"My eyes adjusted, looking through the hole my fingers made. In the distance, I saw something. Three shadows." Ursula stopped. Why was she telling Jill this? The words came out automatically, but she didn't want to be saying them.

"Did you recognise any of the figures?" Jill's question came out too smoothly.

"Figures?"

The word floated out of Ursula's mouth like a bubble and popped into the room. Each second stretched, as she waited for an answer.

"The three people with you in the desert," Jill continued, calm as always. "Did you see their faces, or could you think of their names?"

Time slowed around Ursula. She had only said they were shadows.

Jill must have known there would be three people in the desert before Ursula ever saw them. The clarity was almost blinding as all the pieces fell into place. Ursula could see it now: Ms Swaiteck, the door, the notepad... They were only the most recent parts of the story. From the start Jill had been shrugging off these painful flashes, insisting they weren't anything to worry about. Jill must know what was happening and, based on what Ursula had seen, so did the founder of Swan.

Her soul crashed back into her body. The lights were brighter. The sound of Jill's breathing was clearer. She could feel the soft clutch of the tissue in her hand.

The how and why of what Jill knew didn't matter now. She needed to get out of there.

"What people?" Ursula forced her muscles to scrunch together in confusion. She hoped she wasn't overdoing it.

"Oh, I'm sorry. When you said shadows, I thought you meant people," Jill recovered smoothly. Her calm unnerved Ursula. "Did these shapes remind you of anything?"

Ursula could sense the test in Jill's question.

"They were more like columns." Ursula hesitated, as if trying to remember. "Maybe cacti? Or rocks? They didn't move."

"Then what happened?"

Had she imagined Jill's eyes squint with disappointment?

"I gasped, and the second I did, the pain came." Ursula lied.

"Right away?" Jill seemed surprised; it was clear she had expected more.

"It happened so fast."

Ursula latched herself onto the strength of her emotional memory, hoping if she could relive it, it might act as a shield. She released the barrier in her chest that had been holding back her panic. The flood of adrenaline rolled through her skin as she tried to remember every second of the gut-wrenching torture she'd felt the evening before. Her muscles tightened from the outside in. Her stomach flattened upward against her spasming oesophagus. It became hard to draw a breath past her mouth.

Jill sprang into recovery mode, guiding Ursula in the usual run of self-soothing exercises. And just as Jill threw the life raft, Ursula realised she needed it. She had taken herself a step too far. Despite all her suspicions about Jill, the therapist was her only anchor now.

Ursula followed Jill's voice back to steady breathing and clear vision, back into the world of lies and madness, uncertainty, and domination. By the time she had recovered, she had drained the time from their session.

It was a relief to get out. The air in the hallway was fresh and cool. Ursula drank it in in large gulps. As her mind cleared, a plan formed. She needed to call Rob.

Mackenzie

Mackenzie hid in the HR department, waiting for the end of Ursula's session. It hadn't been the plan, but she was forced to think on her feet. She hadn't visited the Cygnet 7 building since Ursula's breakdown, so technically a routine check-up was overdue. She honestly didn't have the focus for it, but there was no other reasonable excuse to be in the building. It wasn't like she could go to the commissary and have a quiet coffee. Everyone knew who she was.

So, she made her way down to the fourth floor and claimed she was doing an unscheduled check-in. It would have been usual for her to visit the lab first, but she figured no one would question the boss.

"Good morning, I'm here to see the HR team for an impromptu update and feedback session," Mackenzie lied smoothly, keeping her face a perfect neutral,

The man at the desk's eyes grew wide.

"Where is best to meet everyone?" Mackenzie asked before he could answer.

"Um. I am so sorry, Ms Swaiteck, I don't have anything on the calendar."

"That's the impromptu part," Mackenzie pulled out her most winning smile.

"I'm not here to interrupt anyone in the middle of something," she continued, "I just try to drop in a few times a year to meet with each department and receive feedback. Just let Myra and Ajay know. They can round everyone up."

The young man hopped off like a rabbit, leaving Mackenzie to stand by the door. She wavered for a moment, remembering the time. Maybe only one or two people would be in that early.

The young man came back, his face much more composed, and led Mackenzie to a table in one of the glass-box offices.

Thankfully, the HR team put in early days so they could leave for the school run, and all ten members of the team were excited to spend time with the boss. Under the guise of turning her phone on silent, Mackenzie noted the time on the screensaver. She would need to kill at least an hour. She then turned to the assembled group – all grinning to various degrees – and nodded.

"So, what things are working, what isn't, and how can we make it better?" she asked.

The table exploded with chatter. She didn't need to worry about waiting an hour, she realised. It would be harder to keep it that short.

Most of the ideas passed like clouds, distant and unobserved. Under her feigned interest, Mackenzie berated herself for coming to Jill's office at all. It had seemed like a promising idea this morning, when Jill was anxiously wringing her hands, unable to eat anything. She thought her presence would be comforting, and Jill was able to talk out her nerves before Ursula arrived.

Mackenzie bit back the irony of her best intentions. All she had wanted to do this morning was to be there for the woman she loved. Especially after storming out the night before. Instead, it presented yet another avenue for Ursula to divide them. She could no longer walk her partner to the office without risking everything. That risk, too, was born of the best intentions. From the start, she had tried to do the right thing with Ursula, despite not being sure what the right thing was.

She had brought Ursula home, and included Jill, to protect her. To give her a place to live and hide, where she wasn't afraid. They had, briefly, become friends. There was nothing Mackenzie wanted more than for things to be that simple again.

But it was only simple because Ursula wasn't supposed to be around for long. They expected to hide her for a few days, maybe weeks, but when she stayed, the possibility of being caught became real. All their lives became dangerous simply through existing. Burying her in the layers of the company had been another clumsy attempt to help. At the time, it seemed like the safest option. She and Jill had decided on that course of action together. Both in agreement and both playing their part. It felt like a family decision, and one that gave Ursula her own, independent, normal life (or, normal for a walking scientific breakthrough).

It worked, briefly. Then Ursula's mind started to unravel. And again, Jill and Mackenzie were called on for their best intentions – only, this time, Jill took charge. Jill had been the one to decide on hypnosis and was the one to execute it. She should have realised from that point on there was a growing divide between her and the duo of Jill and Ursula: Doctor and Patient. There was no 'doctor, patient, and wife'. Suddenly, the best Mackenzie could offer was to keep away.

Distance had been a key component of their plan. If they could provide Ursula with a break from the past, there was a chance she could move on and have a healthy new life. The hypnosis altering her memory had been one essential piece to the puzzle. The other, Jill insisted, was a completely fresh start. Mackenzie had done all she could to facilitate that. She bought a flat for Ursula in a new town; one by the water that she had always dreamed of. She had designed a new job and entirely new department in Swan. She designed and installed specialty locks and built a room into Jill's office so the past could be sealed away. Mackenzie had even gone so far as to agree to her own exclusion. After all, Jill reminded her, an employee of Swan wouldn't be on a first-name basis with the owner of the company.

And look where it had all led.

Mackenzie struggled to keep a grimace off her face. Running into Ursula again at such a precarious moment felt like an omen. The memory of it landed like lead in her lungs.

Her thoughts – and the meeting – were disrupted by one of the assistants, who popped his head in to remind one of the HR team that they had a meeting at 9:30. Urgently aware that 90 minutes had passed, Mackenzie used the interruption to wrap up the meeting up and dole out her handshakes. It must have been a banner day for the Cygnet 7 HR team; she had agreed without any questions to community volunteering, more vegan dessert options in the café, a monthly free yoga session, and one or two other ideas she couldn't remember.

She rushed up the stairs to the sixth floor and opened Jill's door without knocking. Her partner, slumped over her desk, didn't bother to look up when Mackenzie entered. The sight made her numb.

"You were right," Jill groaned into her desk. "Ursula shouldn't have been coming to this office."

"Did she find it?" Mackenzie asked, her voice steadier than her pirouetting heart.

"I think so. Maybe… I don't know," Jill looked up, her eyes wild and lost, like a child.

"What happened?" Mackenzie asked. She slumped into a chair, her legs unable to support her body any longer.

Jill's words tumbled out in half-formed sentences, jumbling over one another in uncertainty. Mackenzie managed to establish that while Ursula was describing her latest vision to Jill, she suddenly stopped speaking and was staring at the wall about where the door would be. After that, Ursula's behaviour was strange, and she had a panic attack. The facts didn't seem damning, but the way Jill was speaking unnerved Mackenzie.

"Take a breath." Mackenzie tried to muster her strength and send it to Jill. "Did Ursula say anything about the door?"

"No," Jill shook her head weakly. "But she stared at the floor, right where the door meets the carpet. I could tell that she was distracted by something. She must have seen it."

"Ursula couldn't have seen anything from here." Mackenzie reassured her. "I can't see any hint of the door, and I'm looking for it."

"She wasn't sitting there. She was closer to the wall." Jill flung her arm out aimlessly. Mackenzie guessed she was gesturing at the window.

"You can see the metal lip on the underside of the door from where she was. At some angles, you can see the outline. Believe me."

Mackenzie cursed.

"How certain are you that she saw the door?" She asked urgently. "90 percent?"

"Less than that," Jill took a long breath. "Probably only 60-40. That moment when she stopped speaking, I almost felt certain she was looking at it. But the rest of the session, Ursula didn't look back to the door. She was rattled and jumpy, but she didn't seem suspicious of me."

"Okay, that's a positive. Did she keep telling you about the memory?" Mackenzie asked. She tried to recreate the scene in her head. Maybe Jill was overreacting.

"Yeah, she did keep talking," Jill's brow relaxed. "She mentioned seeing shadows, so she must have still trusted me. And she was so vulnerable. You should have seen her shaking when she talked about the pain."

"This sounds like good news," Mackenzie ventured.

"How is a patient hyperventilating good news?" Anger edged back into Jill's voice.

"I didn't mean Ursula getting upset," Mackenzie groaned. She could feel her patience shredded.

"What I was saying – if you would allow anyone else to weigh in on your precious patient – is that if Ursula was still trusting you with her vision, then she may not have noticed the door. Or, if she saw the door, that it didn't trigger anything." Mackenzie's jaw was tight by the time she finished explaining.

"You aren't listening to me," Jill sputtered.

Mackenzie had expected an argument, or more yelling, but Jill was fighting back tears. The change in her voice made Mackenzie sit upright.

"If you could get past your childish jealousy, you could hear that I am saying you were right," she continued. "It doesn't matter if she remembered today. She will at some point, and probably soon. I can't help her, not in this office."

Tears finally took over. Jill smothered her face with her hands but drops still trickled off her chin.

Mackenzie found the strength in her legs to stand and go to her partner. Kneeling beside the chair she tried to wrap an arm over Jill's waist. As she did, Jill howled and rested her head on her partner's shoulder. The despair was palpable, filling the room and draining any resistance from Mackenzie.

"This is a disaster," Jill gulped through her tears. "There's nothing I can do."

Feeling Jill shake in her arms, Mackenzie released herself to the waves of bitterness and exhaustion. Their lives felt like they were no longer their own. Mackenzie found herself wishing that Ursula had died, as expected. She could be a fond memory now, remembered as a foundation for some of the beautiful things in their life.

Was she a monster for thinking that?

She knew she should be grateful. Ursula had made Mackenzie's work possible, had made Swan possible, and had given all of them a future. But it had come at such a great personal cost.

Despairing, Mackenzie looked to the sky wishing for the divine intervention she knew was not there. Feeling the nothingness around them, Mackenzie forced herself to speak.

"It's okay," she reassured Jill. Her voice sounded foreign to her ears.

"How?" Jill wailed.

"We know we can't run from this anymore. We know that now." Mackenzie lifted an arm to stoke the back of Jill's head. She had always loved the soft cushioning feel of Jill's curls.

"If we can't fix it, or stop it, or reverse it, there's only one thing left to do."

"We can't," Jill insisted. Her head shot up, beaming at Mackenzie with fear in her eyes. "You said yourself that this could mean the end of Swan. And if it gets out it can mean the end of all of us."

"Swan will probably have to collapse, but we will go to Ursula first. And we'll find a better way to let the truth out. All three of us. Whatever happens, I will do everything I can to keep us alive and safe."

Jill hesitated.

"Ursula too," Mackenzie reassured her.

"We can't," Jill pleaded. "That's why we didn't do this months ago. Or when she first appeared. You knew from the start that the government wouldn't let something like this get out. There's nothing you can do to protect us. It's impossible."

"We've done everything we can think of. It's time for the unthinkable." Mackenzie gave a weak smile.

"Oh God," Jill moaned and leaned back into Mackenzie's shoulder. But in her voice, Mackenzie, also heard a hint of relief.

She felt her muscles unwind. This was the only way. She knew it in her bones. They couldn't hide the truth any longer.

"First, though, let's go home," Mackenzie said. "We both need some rest before facing this."

Silently, she thought, *and we deserve one last night before it's over.*

Ursula

A fluorescent light switched on automatically. Ursula froze at the entry to Jill's office, searching for whoever might have turned it on. After a moment, she realised the dimness of the blue-white glow meant it was one of the safety lights.

The angle of the downlight cast abrupt shadows all over the room, giving the appearance that figures were crouched behind every surface. She closed the door firmly and flipped on the overhead light. The fierce yellow glow momentarily blinded her. Once the coloured speckles and shapes faded from her vision, she took in the room.

Without the pleasant spread of sunlight or Jill's comforting presence, the room felt sterile. The grey of the couch seemed artificial, a manufactured simulacrum of comfort rather than a cosy collection of cushions, worn with time. The art on the walls reflected the harsh, cold glow of the fluorescent in wide wedges of white. The room was both sterile and defensive.

Ursula forced herself not to be distracted by the strangeness of it. Rob had warned her that, with his ID card, she would only have fifteen minutes before the night guard appeared, maybe twenty. When he gave her his access card, that seemed like plenty of time, but now she realised how short her window was.

It was a struggle to find the seam of the hidden door along the wall. The angle of the sunlight in the afternoon must have been exactly right to catch on the sliver of metal. Now, lit only by the main light, the carpet appeared to blend seamlessly into the edges of the room.

No wonder I hadn't seen it before, she thought.

Guessing at the exact location behind Jill's desk, Ursula crouched down and ran her finger along the edge of the carpet, searching for the feel of smooth metal. She felt her way along nearly to the corner before doubling back toward the bookcase.

It took three passes before her fingers caught on the smooth steel lip barely protruding from the wall. It was cold to the touch.

She traced the lip until it met the vertical seam marking the door's edge. Despite being centimetres away, the seam was easier to feel than it was to see. Using her fingernails as a guide, Ursula moved her hands slowly upwards until, a few feet from the ground, they jammed with a biting sting.

"Acchh," Ursula grunted softly. She shook her hands to throw off the jamming pain. When it faded to an ache, she returned to the task. Her fingers fumbled as she tried to relocate the slit. After a moment she gave up and ran her palm over the area. As she swept across the wall, she thought she felt something graze the base of her palm.

She followed the line carefully with her fingertips and realised it outlined a small rectangle in the middle of the wall. Instinctively, Ursula pushed. A section of the wall sunk beneath her fingertips, forming a narrow recess that created a handle within the wall. Fitted within the handle, she knew, would be the fingerprint reader Rob had repaired.

She leaned forward and spotted the black surface lining the underside of the handle, where one's fingers would curve around it to open the door. The angle wasn't ideal, but she could easily feel the raised edges of its outline. She hoped that would be enough.

Ursula searched her pockets for the other gift from Rob: a small key, no wider than the barrel of a paperclip, designed to trigger on all of Swan's keypads. Holding the key between her teeth, she reached in and ran her fingers over the frictionless surface. There were no grooves of holes that she could feel. She tried grazing the surface in another direction, but again it was smooth.

In frustration she clenched her hand around the handle. A familiar beep sounded from within the wall. She looked down to see blue light cast over her wrist, indicating that the scanner was reading.

Her first thought was to let go. The fingerprint lock would keep a digital log of who attempted access. But, by now, it already had her fingerprints. No alarms had sounded, and the light hadn't immediately turned red. After a beat, the colour went green, and the sound of pressure releasing hissed from all sides of the door before it released, opening fractionally into the room.

For a moment Ursula could only stare. There was no good reason why her fingerprints should unlock the door. Her lips parted in surprise, causing Rob's key to fall to the floor. She heard the tinkle of metal on metal and a faint rolling of the key on a hard floor.

Ursula pulled open the door to follow it, setting off another set of automatic lights. The cold light gave her pause. She hovered half-in the door as she took in the space before her. It was larger than she expected – perhaps twice the size – but was designed to fit no more than two people. The walls were painted an industrial, cheap white, and the ceiling was lit with a single row of bare fluorescent bulbs. It was anonymous and sterile.

Ursula's heart sunk at the sight of the largely empty space. There wasn't a computer in sight.

The only furnishings seemed to be a shelving unit directly in front of her. Taking up two-thirds of the wall it was a metal framework of shelves and drawers in office beige. Against the starkness of the walls, it appeared muddy. The top two shelves were occupied by the thin black plastic of generic DVD covers ending with two silver and white hard drives.

She approached the shelves for a closer look. It didn't make sense for her files, or anything tied to the Medusa and its Reader, to be on DVDs. The technology was outmoded.

She pulled out one of the DVDs and read the looped handwriting carefully written on the cover. Each was labelled 'therapy session' with a date beneath. She looked at two more. They were organised by date, going back at least five years. The hard drives didn't have any labels on them, but they didn't need to.

Embarrassment burnt in Ursula's cheeks, clashing with the cool of the surrounding room. Sage had been right. This was a secure storage closet for patient files. There was no sign of anything secret or sinister about it. It had been the most logical, sensible solution. Jill's voice rang in her head with the distant chant of 'Occam's razor'.

Shame quickly turned to a flutter of humiliation as the seriousness of what she'd done settled into her chest. There was no reasonable explanation for why she had broken into her therapist's office and accessed private patient files. Her throat spasmed. It struck her that she didn't have a full understanding of what she had expected to find. It had been a hunch. Paranoia. A series of moments connected only in the wild imaginings of her mind.

They were going to commit her this time, she realised. She had gone too far. Or worse – they might not believe her story. Given her history, they should, but what she had done could be seen as corporate espionage, or maybe attempted blackmail. They would have to fire her, or have her arrested, or both.

Ursula covered her mouth against the curdled taste in her tongue. Maybe she could run? The thought floundered the moment it arose. The lock already had her fingerprints.

The lock. The sickly sensation was replaced with a shiver of ice down her spine. It had opened with her fingerprints. She hadn't broken into the file room; she had been admitted.

But why?

Something in here must belong to her; must be something she needed access to. Maybe it was her patient files, but that seemed unlikely. Maybe her instinct had been right. Maybe Rob was right. She was allowed in here because she was part of the Medusa experiment. That had to be the only explanation, she just needed to find the evidence.

Ursula stepped back and scanned the shelf again. A long drawer at waist height seemed to call to her. It opened in a smooth roll. Someone must have oiled it because it didn't make a sound. She peered inside and swayed at the strange wave of déjà vu. In the drawer lay three objects, carefully arranged on a white, cushioned surface. They stared back at her like old friends.

At the centre of the arrangement was the all-too familiar steampunk squid that made up the Medusa machine. It was arranged with the cap to the right and the array of cables laid carefully out to the left, like a resting head with hair cascading over the pillow. It must have been an early prototype because there was none of the usual white coating to the wires. Each one was a dirty grey with signs of wear at the connection points, which were patched in black electrical tape that curled up at the edges. The cap itself was frayed and worn. On a closer look she realised it was made of plain grey cloth. A pull beneath her ribs made Ursula aware she felt inexplicably sad for the object.

She followed the line of the cables as they reached towards the nearest object like a mechanical nightmare of Michelangelo's "The Creation of Adam". On the receiving end of the gesture was a metal box partly encased in plastic that anyone would recognise as a console. Attached to it by thin grey wires were two black strips like bandages with embedded wires, and a black disk as round and spongey as the one she so often fitted to her neck.

Ursula smiled. It must be her Reader. A primitive, unimpressive version of the one in her room, it only had three sensor relays and none of them looked particularly safe. Ursula reached out gently and ran her fingers over the dented covering. Someone must have dropped it. She wondered if it still worked.

Probably not, she reasoned. Both pieces looked ragged compared to the sleek versions she knew, and not merely in design. The cap to the Medusa and the ankle sensors of the Reader had tears in the material and bits of cloth sticking out wildly at the edges. The dent in the Reader was as large as her fist, and the impact had been forceful enough to wrench the corner from its welding. The internal damage was bound to be extensive.

She shifted to the third object: a short metal pole. At first glance, she hadn't been as drawn to it. It was as familiar as the other two, but it could be recognised by anyone. The carbon converters were now painted green, but otherwise the model apparently didn't need any improving.

She picked the converter up and rolled it around in her hands. Close up there were obvious signs of corrosion along the joins, and wear over the surface. In places there were streaks of shining metal, suggesting that flecks of something hard had glanced off the surface at great speed.

Ursula bit her lip. Swan was only four years old, and yet the signs of damage and wear made the objects look like artefacts from the past. It didn't make sense.

She placed the converter back in the drawer and closed it. For a while she stood there, waiting for understanding to dawn on her. Once again, she hadn't found what she was looking for, but it added to the unsolvable puzzle before her.

There was a Medusa machine in here – which she had expected – but it was old, and she doubted it could be used. There wasn't any sign of a computer, any storage for her notes, or anything else to suggest Swan was experimenting on her. The only sign of her in the room at all was among the archive of patient files Jill had saved. And alongside those patient files were rare original designs for the most famous technology on the planet, and Cygnet 7's top-secret machine.

The pieces were all laid out before her, but she couldn't make any of them fit. She could understand why the first prototype of the Medusa would be in the building where it was being perfected – but shouldn't it be in a lab? Why would this equipment be with patient files? Why did they seem worn and overused if the technology was only four years old?

And why did her fingerprints unseal a door that was filled with sensitive material?

She had added to her list of questions, but not the answers. There was no sign that Jill knew about the desert, and no suggestion that anything in that room, aside from the fingerprint reader, was meant for her.

I'm going mad.

The realisation made her feel tired and cold. Ursula's vision went fuzzy with tears. She turned to leave, but she couldn't see through the cascade. Her eyes stung as she clenched them, but it didn't stop the overflow. Blindly she felt her way towards the door. Her face was hot, as was her chest and her legs. The burning was growing unbearable. She needed to get out. She needed air. Her lungs scraped and she choked on a mix of phlegm and tears. She groped for the open door.

Her hand connected with something soft.

Gulping, she tried to scrape the tears away with her fingers. The vision was still glistening at the edges, but she was able to make out a silhouette.

Someone was here.

She cried out, the tears sputtering out of her eyelids. She grabbed at the guard. But there was no bulk. It was cloth. She blinked away the tears trying to focus on what was in front of her. She realised she was beside the doorway and, there hanging before her, was the cloth outline of a suit.

Bewildered, she yanked the bodysuit off its hanger. The material flexed but did not catch, slipping into her waiting hands in a shimmering waterfall of black and blue. Up close, she could see the details of each smooth scale, dark as obsidian and mailable as plastic. She rubbed the material between her fingers and recognised its skin-like softness; it felt just as it had in the desert.

A noise from the outer office made her jump. Ursula stepped out in time to see Jill enter the lit room. The therapist's eyes went straight for Ursula. Her face was serene and calm, as though she expected to find her patient in the closet doorway.

Ursula wanted to curse or scream but felt choked by emotion. The mix of embarrassment, shame, anger, and fear ran by too quickly for her to anchor onto one. All she could manage was a gurgling amid the tracks of tears and snot.

"Good evening, Ursula." Jill said, breaking the silence.

The composed greeting managed to crystalise Ursula's anger.

"Where did you get this?" Ursula growled, holding up the bodysuit.

Jill moved to take a step forward and then stopped herself. She looked back silently at Ursula, her gaze steady but sad. The mocking sympathy stung.

"This is from the desert," Ursula shook the bodysuit at her, strangling it. "How do you have this?"

Jill's eyes widened but she didn't speak.

"You never thought it was a dream, did you Jill?" Ursula spat. "It wasn't the machine, or anxiety, or meditation, it was real. It's all been real."

Ursula found herself shaking violently. She tried to get her body under control, but it spasmed with each effort. Tears were streaming now. She could feel them drop from her chin to her chest and soak into her shirt.

"Tell me," Ursula raged, her voice gurgling. "Tell me what you are doing to me! Is this some kind of experiment?"

Jill opened her mouth and closed it again. Ursula felt pummelled by the silence. Her head swayed and clenched. The floor undulated around her.

"If this suit is real, then the desert is real." Ursula tried to anchor herself with her words, fighting a growing faintness. "I deserve to know..."

Her knees buckled. By some inhuman force she managed to lunge for the desk and right herself. She could hear someone's footsteps moving towards her. Adrenaline allowed her to lift her head up in time to watch Jill approach.

"Stop," she growled before her head drooped back down.

Jill stopped.

Ursula heaved a few breaths to try and keep the world from spinning. Through the dizziness she forced herself to look up.

"You gave that suit to me," Jill finally replied, "a long time ago."

The therapist's voice was trembling. Her eyes were narrowed with worry. Ursula swelled with defiance at the false mockery of empathy.

"Lies," Ursula cried out hysterically. "More lies. Lies and then lies, and then lies."

The world was steady again, but it shifted its giddiness into her. Her body felt like it was fluttering out of control, bringing her along for a swerving, drunken ride.

"I have never seen anything like this before. Not until I had those visions." Ursula continued.

"Well –" Jill started.

"You have been lying to me," Ursula screamed. The world snapped into focus. Her entire body clenched. She felt her anger squeezing from every pore in her body.

"I trusted you, and you lied."

"I'm not lying Ursula," Jill pleaded. "It's complicated."

"It's my *life,*" Ursula screamed and threw the suit to the floor. "You have been telling me not to worry about these trips to the desert, but it turns out I should have been very worried. What are you doing to me? Are you transporting me from the desert in some psychic tractor beam? Is it psychological torture? How much of it is real and how much is in my mind?"

The questions ran into one another, falling from Ursula's mind until her breath stopped. As she listed every mad, fractured idea, none sounded real. It was impossible. For the first time, she hoped Jill would say she was going mad.

"It's all real," Jill insisted. "But all of it happened in the distant past, Ursula."

Ursula swayed. She felt light again.

"Your visions," Jill continued "I thought you had already realised they were memories."

"Memories?" Ursula repeated.

The word was the gong in Ursula's mind sounding the retreat on all emotion. Hatred, dread, and suffering all washed down to her feet and bled into the carpet.

"I thought you saw the door in your last session," Jill confessed. "I assumed when you did, the memories would come flooding back and you would realise that you have been to the desert. That you lived there, long before we met."

"I've never seen a desert before. I've never left Britain before," Ursula said, but her words came out sounding uncertain.

She strained to reach back into her past. She could barely remember her father's face, with a long nose jutting out over a greying beard. Was he standing in a desert? Or was he in a flat? When she was little, wasn't she always complaining about being thirsty?

"You did Ursula," Jill's voice scattered the loose threads of the image. "Try to remember. It was your home."

"I don't remember." Ursula leaned against the desk for support.

"Don't focus on when you were young; it may be too long ago," Jill soothed. "Think of your visions. Doesn't the desert seem familiar to you? Didn't you say that, before the pain, you felt at peace there."

Ursula shook her head. For a while the desert had felt like home. But that was after seeing several images of it. At first all she felt was pain and fear.

Jill looked wildly around the room, searching for something. Suddenly she pointed past Ursula with urgency.

"You have been in that room before," she declared. "Look at the suit, look at everything in that room; don't they seem familiar?"

Ursula rolled her upper body back toward the closet. She remembered the feeling of connection she had with the Medusa. But the rest of the room had felt alien.

"You chose what you wanted to keep and put it in that room yourself," Jill pressed on. "Right down to the lock which can only be opened with your fingerprints."

Ursula glanced down at her left hand and the fingerprints that registered on the machine. Now, they seemed like a stranger's.

"But…" Ursula struggled to form a sentence. In the end only two words came out: "Your office."

"With your closet. You asked me to keep it safe." Jill's voice was soft as satin, gently winding itself around Ursula. She felt an immediate urge to resist it.

"No." Ursula's mind skipped like a record. "That can't be right."

The sound of footsteps hit her ears. A surge of adrenaline shot her upward.

"Who else is there?" Ursula demanded; her voice still cracked.

Jill sighed and looked over to the door. Ursula followed her gaze to watch the founder of Swan enter.

"Hi Urs," Mackenzie said with an uncomfortable smile.

"What are you doing here?" Ursula exclaimed.

"When that door opens," Mackenzie nodded the closet, "Jill and I both get an alert. You set it up that way."

"Bullshit," Ursula gritted her teeth. "I wouldn't know how to set up something like this. You two probably got an alert the same way security does when someone comes onto this floor. That has nothing to do with me."

Now they were both lying to her. It didn't make sense. What would be the point? She looked back at Jill, but she was still looking at Ursula with tragedy in her eyes.

Jill opened her mouth to speak but Mackenzie cut her off.

"Security doesn't have access to that door," Mackenzie stated calmly.

Ursula was gripped by the truth of what she said. Rob had told her that the hidden door was not part of the main security system.

"Okay," Ursula swallowed. "But that doesn't matter. The point is that I didn't set up anything, you did."

"You didn't, literally, put the system together," Mackenzie admitted. "But it was you who asked for this room to be hidden and locked so that only you could access it. The only other condition was that Jill and I to come if you ever opened it."

"Stop!" Ursula screamed. She felt her frustration press against her lungs. It was too much. She needed them to stop. She needed everything to stop. Her mind screamed for a way out.

"I don't know anything about Cygnet!" Ursula wailed. "I've barely worked here for two years."

"Four actually." There was a bitterness in Mackenzie's words. It cut at Ursula.

"Think about it, Ursula," Jill's soft voice floated across the room. Her gentleness made a jarring contrast to Mackenzie's clipped tones.

"Just using logic, go through it in your own mind. How did you manage to open that door?"

"The fingerprint lock," Ursula mumbled.

"Therefore, you must, at the very least, have given a fingerprint reading to that particular lock."

"Stop trying to confuse me," Ursula begged. Her head throbbed. She raised her hands to her head. With a sick shock she realised she was massaging the same spot that hurt when she had her first vision.

"We aren't trying to make things worse. But we need you to accept the truth," Jill pleaded.

"Occam's razor!" Ursula sputtered. "It's your constant refrain. The simplest explanation is always the right one. There is nothing simple about what you are saying."

"That's because there is nothing simple about you, Ursula," Jill insisted, keeping her voice soft. "Or what's happening to you. You're remembering things that none of us have ever seen before."

"These aren't memories!" Ursula's throat and limbs scalded with frustration. She screamed to the ceiling. This couldn't be happening.

"I have never been to a desert before. I had never seen that suit before my visions. This is technology I couldn't imagine. It's light years ahead of me, ahead of anyone."

"It is light years ahead of us," Mackenzie boomed. "Which is why you had to bring it back. They are your memories, Ursula, but they are also *our* future."

Ursula felt the room pitch.

"Every piece of technology in that closet – the Medusa, the carbon converter, that suit – they are *yours*. You brought the carbon converter back to us... to me." Mackenzie's words barrelled through her.

"You wanted to save the world. You see, in your time the technology came too late. But scientists had guessed early on that by the time a working carbon converter was fully developed, Earth would be a wasteland. And they were right. You told us that when you came from, the population had plummeted, and most of the continents were desert. The only option was for someone to bring it back to a time when it could help. So, you brought it to me, in my lab. I never understood why you picked me, but you did. You gave me the schematics and the prototype."

"You never told us why they chose you," Jill added softly. "But we knew that you were an engineer too. You were able to help Kenzie develop a beta."

"To be fair, at first you didn't realise there would be that kind of time," Mackenzie remarked. "You thought that once you changed the future you would disappear."

"We all did," Jill whispered.

Ursula's tongue felt like lead. She couldn't speak. She couldn't move.

"You were so frightened when you found out you would have to live on in the past," Jill ventured. "In a world so different from the one you knew. We tried to help you assimilate, but you had these awful panic attacks."

"Ursula," Mackenzie took a deep breath and looked at Ursula steadily with her ocean-green eyes.

"You're a time traveller."

Author Biography

Lauren Jane Barnett is a writer, podcaster and indie horror actress best known for *Death Lines: Walking London's Horror History*. Her writing has appeared or is forthcoming in *BFS Horizons, Horrified, Audience Askew* and anthologies including *Tales of Fear, Superstition, and Doom, Error 404,* and *Bloody Good Horror*. She co-hosts London Horror Movie Club podcast alongside her brother, Chris and has been killed in four indie horror movies including *The Witches of the Sands*.

Acknowledgements

I am so incredibly grateful to Cosmic Egg for taking a chance on my first science fiction novella. Thanks to the editorial team for putting this together so people can read it and hopefully find something to love in it. This idea was one that needed many iterations, and to my Spectrum Writers Group, I'm grateful for their time and feedback reading it, especially to Will, John, Rachel, and Kat. Thanks so much to Stephanie Barbir, who always lets me ramble about my ideas, and who believed there was a readership for female-driven Science Fiction – you are the very best friend I could ask for. And, finally, to my inspiration and love, Tony Mardon, who was willing to read this and talk about it too many times; thank you for not letting me give up, and for every day together.

FICTION

Put simply, we publish great stories. Whether it's literary or popular, a gentle tale or a pulsating thriller, the connecting theme in all Roundfire fiction titles is that once you pick them up you won't want to put them down.

If you have enjoyed this book, why not tell other readers by posting a review on your preferred book site.

Recent bestsellers from Roundfire are:

The Bookseller's Sonnets

Andi Rosenthal

The Bookseller's Sonnets intertwines three love stories with a tale of religious identity and mystery spanning five hundred years and three countries.

Paperback: 978-1-84694-342-3 ebook: 978-184694-626-4

Birds of the Nile

An Egyptian Adventure

N.E. David

Ex-diplomat Michael Blake wanted a quiet birding trip up the Nile – he wasn't expecting a revolution.

Paperback: 978-1-78279-158-4 ebook: 978-1-78279-157-7

Blood Profit$

The Lithium Conspiracy

J. Victor Tomaszek, James N. Patrick, Sr.

The blood of the many for the profits of the few… *Blood Profit$* will take you into the cigar-smoke-filled room where American policy and laws are really made.

Paperback: 978-1-78279-483-7 ebook: 978-1-78279-277-2

The Burden

A Family Saga

N.E. David

Frank will do anything to keep his mother and father apart. But he's carrying baggage – and it might just weigh him down …

Paperback: 978-1-78279-936-8 ebook: 978-1-78279-937-5

The Cause

Roderick Vincent

The second American Revolution will be a
fire lit from an internal spark.

Paperback: 978-1-78279-763-0 ebook: 978-1-78279-762-3

Don't Drink and Fly

The Story of Bernice O'Hanlon: Part One

Cathie Devitt

Bernice is a witch living in Glasgow. She loses her way
in her life and wanders off the beaten track looking for the
garden of enlightenment.

Paperback: 978-1-78279-016-7 ebook: 978-1-78279-015-0

Gag

Melissa Unger

One rainy afternoon in a Brooklyn diner, Peter Howland
punctures an egg with his fork. Repulsed, Peter pushes
the plate away and never eats again.

Paperback: 978-1-78279-564-3 ebook: 978-1-78279-563-6

The Master Yeshua

The Undiscovered Gospel of Joseph

Joyce Luck

Jesus is not who you think he is. The year is 75 CE. Joseph
ben Jude is frail and ailing, but he has a prophecy to fulfil ...

Paperback: 978-1-78279-974-0 ebook: 978-1-78279-975-7

On the Far Side, There's a Boy
Paula Coston
Martine Haslett, a thirty-something 1980s woman, plays hard on the fringes of the London drag club scene until one night which prompts her to sign up to a charity. She writes to a young Sri Lankan boy, with consequences far and long.
Paperback: 978-1-78279-574-2 ebook: 978-1-78279-573-5

Tuareg
Alberto Vazquez-Figueroa
With over 5 million copies sold worldwide, *Tuareg* is a classic adventure story from best-selling author Alberto Vazquez-Figueroa, about honour, revenge and a clash of cultures.
Paperback: 978-1-84694-192-4

Readers of ebooks can buy or view any of these bestsellers by clicking on the live link in the title. Most titles are published in paperback and as an ebook. Paperbacks are available in traditional bookshops. Both print and ebook formats are available online.

Find more titles and sign up to our readers' newsletter, visit: www.collectiveinkbooks.com/fiction

Printed and bound by CPI Group (UK) Ltd, Croydon, CR0 4YY
07/01/2025
01816805-0008